unearned
pleasures
AND OTHER STORIES

ursula
hegi

SCRIBNER PAPERBACK FICTION
PUBLISHED BY SIMON & SCHUSTER

SCRIBNER PAPERBACK FICTION
Simon & Schuster Inc.
Rockefeller Center
1230 Avenue of the Americas
New York, NY 10020

First Scribner Paperback Fiction edition 1997
SCRIBNER PAPERBACK FICTION and design are trademarks of Simon & Schuster Inc.

10   9   8   7   6   5   4   3   2   1

Library of Congress Cataloging-in-Publication Data
Hegi, Ursula.
Unearned pleasures and other stories / Ursula Hegi. —1st Scribner Paperback
Fiction ed.
p.   cm.
I. Title.
PR9110.9.H43U5   1997
823—dc21   97-9736
CIP

ISBN 0-684-84485-0

The following stories are reprinted herein with the generous permission of their
original publishers: "To the Gate," PEN Syndication Fiction Project, 1987; "Neah
Bay—Four Miles West," PEN Syndication Fiction Project, 1986; "Other Attics,"
Kayak (January 1981); "Theives," *Feminist Studies* (Summer 1981); "Mushrooms &
Pepperoni & the Woman in This Story," *Kayak* (1979); "Tina's Room," PEN Syn-
dication Fiction Project, 1984; "Where Are You Going?" *Canadian Woman Studies*
(Summer 1982); "Night Voices," *Ms.* (January 1981); "Breaking the Rules," *North
American Review* (forthcoming); "Unearned Pleasures," *Prairie Schooner* (© Univer-
sity of Nebraska Press 1985); "Nobody Stocks Camellias Anymore," *Kayak* (1978);
and "Windows," *Passages North* (forthcoming).

For Susan Wheeler

Contents

To the Gate

AFTERNOONS SHE LEAVES the house that's gray with the smell of her father's dying and heads for the race track, letting the colors, the sounds stab at her: the green of the track, the blue of the hot sky, the red of the flowers.

Shouts: "Come on! Come on ..." — "Get it up! Get it up ..."

Jockeys—sexless and raised above flashes of trembling horseflesh. Cheers. Disappointment. A flurry of tickets on the ground. The rush to the windows to cash in on winners.

She's dizzy from the sun, the noise; yet, she keeps walking. Smells of buttered popcorn. Spilled soda. Hot dogs and ice cream. Young men in red T-shirts: *Saratoga.* Their arms brown, smooth with sweat. She drifts through the grounds, wishing she could feel something. Arms and T-shirts. Red. She brushes her bare arm against that of a man passing her.

No sudden twinge. Like touching a wall. Others. Her flesh against theirs. Skin. Young skin like hers. Nothing.

Nights she lies on the cot outside her father's open door, her head beyond the frame so she won't see his face, only his hands on the blanket, veined and large, too large for his shrunken body. Spots of light brown on his crinkled skin. The gray smell of his cancer has permeated the walls. His breath is shallow. So faint it could stop any moment. And though she can't see his face, it is with her as she lies on the cot, stiffly. His shriveled lips partly open. A pattern of veins on his yellow skull. Like those pictures of emaciated beggars in religious books. This is my father, Elise tells herself, eyes burning, dry. *This is my father who is dying.* Yet, she feels nothing.

Mornings after the nurse arrives, she gets up from the cot. Moves into her room across the hall. Closes the door. Sleeps without dreams. Wakes in the early afternoon to his dying smell, surrounded by things he built for her: the bookshelves, her desk, the windowseat. On the wall his charcoal sketch of the farm in Vermont where he grew up, a cape cod dwarfed by the weathered timbers of the barn.

When she tries to remember what it felt like to love him, she can't. It's as though she were tilted back to the first six years of her life when she felt like a fraud each time her parents told her they loved her. She wasn't sure what it meant—this thing they called love. Whenever she replied, *I love you too,* she was afraid they'd find out and send her away. When, finally, she began to link her feelings to the word love, she felt relieved, grateful.

Lying in her room, weighted by the heat of the August afternoon, she finds it impossible to imagine herself returning to law school. Finds it impossible to imagine anything beyond this summer.

Men in red T-shirts. She walks into their way. Collides with them. Wants the shock of another body against hers. Wants to suck up the energy of the races, the colors, the sounds. Perhaps this is what it's like to be dead—to feel nothing. Yet, she felt after her mother died five years ago: rage, grief, guilt.

The sun burns her bare legs and midriff. She wears her briefest shorts, a blue halter. Sandals. Her hair twisted up to keep her neck free. The grass shimmers under the heat. Shouts. Laughter. Children running. The smell of steamed hot dogs. She eats to service her body. Drinks lemonade that tastes flat. Welcomes the pain in her tooth as she chews the ice. Stares into the sun until everything swims yellow.

When he opens his eyes, they're milky. Clouded. He doesn't recognize her and whimpers when she sets the straw against his lips. Lifting his neck with one hand, she flinches at the touch of his papery skin against her palm. His head lolls back—a limp puppet. His hands move across the blanket as if searching for something.

Only last fall, when he pruned the hedge in front of the house, his hands were steady, his hair full. He wore a chamois shirt that smelled of clean sweat and pipe tobacco. She can't connect that man to him whose face is a nest of bones against the pillow.

The bar is half dark, filled with people though it's only late afternoon. She finds a stool by the bar, orders beer, wanting the bitter taste in her mouth. A man asks her to dance, and she presses against him on the crowded floor, swaying with the music, trying to drown within the noise, the bodies. He brings her tighter against him, runs his hands down her back, her buttocks. Slides them up along the sides of her body to her breasts. She lets him. They dance, his breath heavy, and she wills herself to respond; yet, her feet move automatically, and she finally loosens herself from his arms, knowing it wouldn't change anything if she went to bed with him.

The nurse has prepared a light dinner for her: a salad with pale strips of turkey and cheese spread over the top like a wilting flower.

"You don't need to sleep in the hallway, Elise. Your room's close enough."

"I might not hear him."

The nurse is a kind woman, a tall woman with wide wrists who likes to earn overtime. "Stay as long as you want to," she encourages Elise every afternoon. And she advises her, "Hang around the fifty dollar window. That's where the pros bet. I always do before I take my money to the two dollar window."

But now she walks from the house, and Elise watches her through the kitchen window, the white of her uniform, of her shoes and stockings, until she gets into her car, a bright red Toyota. Upstairs, in the silence, *he* is waiting for her to watch him die. Her legs feel heavy as she walks up the steps and stands in the open door of his room. His nose juts from his sunken features; yet, his chest still rises with each breath. Nothing has changed. His hairless skull yellow in the dim light. His hands like broken birds on the blanket.

Lying on the cot, she tries to replay the colors of the track, the sounds, the body of the man in the bar. Yet, everything has faded as though it had happened inside this house. Her father's breath is faint, so faint that sometimes she thinks it has stopped. But, straining for it, she hears it again. It's almost dawn when a familiar voice startles her.

"Three feet to the west…" *His* voice. Strong. "From this point 230 feet straight to the gate post."

Somewhere, within his decades of memories, her father is walking the property line of the farm in Vermont. She remembers the gate post. Weathered. Smooth. There was no gate, but at the other end of the post stood a picket fence. As a child she spent summers on the farm. Until her grandparents died and it was sold.

"And from the gate post twenty-eight rods up the hill to the granite marker."

She pictures him in heavy boots, counting his steps as he walks uphill through a low stand of pines in the frosty morning air, measuring the land he knows so well. His voice is steady, that of a man who knows his territory, who takes pride in the land he returned to every summer with his children, the land he helped his father clear, muscles swelling on his arms as he lifted cut lengths of timer.

"From the granite marker south…" His voice rises. "…to the brook."

The brook where she piled rocks into a dam, sectioned off a small basin to sail the boats he made for her from twigs and leaves. She couldn't see the house from the brook. Only meadows. Clumps of grass to her ankles. Her heart beating, she waits for her father's voice to take her down the wide dirt road through the orchard, past the shed with the ciderpress.

She finds herself standing by his bed, leaning over him, wanting to keep him connected to his memories. Her memories. "The orchard. We're walking though the orchard..."

But his voice has stopped. His eyes are closed, and his breath catches each time he exhales. Yet, only moments ago he was free, striding the boundaries of his parents' land, deciding
his own direction.

Lifting his head, she carefully supports it with one hand while raising his pillow. Now his breath comes easier. The blanket above his chest rises. Falls. Rises. A blue vein pulses in his temple.

Her throat aching, she whispers, "The ciderpress. Remember the smell of the apples?"

His lips move.

She draws closer.

"Three feet to the west..." He has returned to where he started out. "From this point 230 feet straight to—" He moans. His fingers pluck the blanket.

She lays her right hand over his frail fingers. They tremble. Then yield to her touch and rest. His skin is warm. Dry. "To the gate post," she urges him on.

"To the gate post. And from the gate post 28 rods up the hill..." Her father's voice swells. Fills the room. "... to the granite marker. From the granite marker south ... to the brook..."

Neah Bay—Four Miles West

THE OLD WOMAN who runs the pink motel paints seascapes in childlike forms; they cover the walls of the five motel rooms that block the view of the sea from the small house where she lives with her husband, a house that reeks with the odor of too many cats.

I've come to this beach with my daughter, Kathryn, after spending the summer without her. My last summer before I turn forty, and my lover is drawing away from me. He wants to get married and is beginning to believe me that I don't want to get married again. A week before my daughter returned, he cried in my arms when he told me that he is forcing himself to stay away from me. I feel fragile. Raw. Try not to cling to him.

I convince my daughter to go beach scavenging with me. She'll be thirteen the end of September, less than a month away, but she looks older in her tight black skirt and purple shirt which her father let her buy. Huge pieces of driftwood—entire trees—lie on the sand above the high tide mark. Jagged and bleached, they remind me of dinosaur bones. When I touch them, they feel like silk. We pick up cone shaped shells and stones that are hollowed and smoothed by the waves.

Inside her largest stone Kathryn finds a shell which she can't pry out with her red fingernails, and for a moment she's almost as enthusiastic as she used to be before she left last June. "The snail must have climbed inside the hole when it was quite small," she tells me, "but then it got too large to get out and finally died."

The stone is smooth, reddish, and looks like one of Picasso's sculptures—rounded and fertile. For a while she carries it, but then she drops it back on the sand. When I bend to pick it up, she shakes her head as if impatient with me. Since it's too big to fit into the pockets of my windbreaker with the shells, I cradle it in my arms.

Soon Kathryn grows bored and returns to our room to read the *Glamour* magazine she bought in Seattle while we waited for the ferry. On the stretch of beach below the motel the old woman's husband has piled up twigs and split logs of tamarack above the charred remains of a fire. I sit down on a piece of driftwood next to it. Early this morning—it wasn't even five yet when I woke up and looked out of the window—I saw him and the old woman on the beach. They looked like oversized children. She stood behind her easel, a brush raised in one hand, gazing across the strait as if seeing the scene she's painted so often for the first time. Wind raised her thin, white hair from the collar of the cardigan that hung loosely from her massive shoulders. The old man—a hunter's vest over his plaid shirt—carefully laid the firewood into a pyramid shape. When he finished, he walked over to her and, his shoulder almost touching hers, looked in the same direction.

Digging my toes into the cold sand, I watch the light changing to the mauves and pinks of evening. My daughter has spent two months with her father in Colorado. I've never been away from her this long. All summer I've looked forward to our vacation, imagining us by the edge of the water, laughing, running, perhaps playing chase, our feet whipping the shallow surf into a fine spray, our voices soaring into the air that's rich with the smell of salt and tamarack and kelp. But Kathryn doesn't like the motel, the beach, the swarms of spotted kittens that rub against our ankles and try to dart into our room when we unlock the door. She has told me the old woman looks like a witch with her tooth stumps and the white whiskers that sprout from her upper lip. When I hugged Kathryn at the airport, she seemed embarrassed. Despite my objections she wears make-up and clothes that make her look like a little hooker.

I feel ashamed of that thought, but I can't help it. When she left, her blond hair hung down her back; now it's cropped short except for a skinny tail in back of her neck which she dyed black in Colorado. When she asked me last spring if she could wear her hair like that, I wouldn't let her. Maybe I should have. I'm not sure. From what I gather, she was left alone most days while her father went to his office. He gave her money for food, for the movies, for clothes, but when he came home one evening and found what she'd done to her hair, he phoned me to say how disappointed he was with her choices.

I've been careful not to mention her hair at all. Careful with other things too. Like not being silly the way we used to be together. Or not giving her hugs though I want to. There's something plastic about her. Brittle, almost. As if she might break. She holds her arms close to her body, hardly speaks, and avoids looking into my eyes. Many girls her age dress and behave like that—I know, I see them in the hallways of Kathryn's school or at the clinic when their mothers bring them in to my office for check-ups or advice about birth control. It doesn't help to remind myself of that. In not too many years Kathryn will have left me. Though I've tried to prepare myself for that, I suddenly feel it has already happened. It's much too soon. For her too, I believe.

The reddish stone she found is resting on my knees, and I run one hand across its smooth surface, circling the hole where the shell is wedged. Last night I dreamed I gave birth to another daughter. Lying on the bed below one of the old woman's seascapes, I delivered the child myself. Without effort or pain I reached across my swollen belly and between my thighs, guiding the small, moist head, then her body from my depths—a service I've performed for countless women. It felt right that I would do it for myself. I held her in my arms. Drew her toward my breasts. When I woke up I remembered my dream with a rush of joy though I've known for a long time that I don't want another child.

A wide ribbon of fog has risen from the strait of Juan de Fuca and hides the lower half of the mountains on Vancouver Island across the water. Four miles west from here is Neah Bay, the Makah Indian reservation, where rows of unpainted shacks cling to the edge of a magnificent crescent-shaped beach. A wide band of piled up stones separates the harbor from the open sea. No Holiday Inn, no MacDonald's, no mini-golf course to spoil the scenery. Hand-lettered signs point toward Cape Flattery, the point furthest west and north in the U.S. The largest building in town is an alcohol rehabilitation center. This afternoon Kathryn and I drove into Neah Bay to find croissants for tomorrow's breakfast. Thin dogs without collars sniffed the cement in front of the only store. The clerk, a short woman with wide features and black bangs, did not smile when she rung up the boxed doughnuts we'd found on the bread shelf. In her flat eyes, my reflection looked too blond. Too tall.

The old woman's husband comes around the side of the motel with a can of charcoal lighter. His plaid flannel shirt is faded and worn. He walks slowly as if conscious of each step.

"To keep you warm," he says and smiles at me.

From the can he squirts a clear thread of liquid over the pile of wood, tosses a lit match into it, and shuffles back toward the buildings as the fire rises in two columns like the wings of a prehistoric bird. The old woman and her husband look like they have been together for many years. I will never have that. Did not want that. At least not with Kathryn's father who gave me long-suffering looks whenever I wanted to play.

My lover has told me he wishes he met me twenty years ago. Before I married. Before he married for the first time. I admire and question his courage. I'm moved by his belief that we would still be together. Though I told him that I didn't want to marry again, he imagined us together. Forever. Like his parents who hold hands when they go for walks. Who travel all over the world. Who take classes together in photography and sculpture.

I've cried for him because, after growing up with parents whose love has grown, his two marriages have ended in divorce. Yet, I cannot give him the permanence he wants. I would have liked to keep living in separate places, seeing each other when both of us chose to. But he is forcing himself not to need me, so that he can look for the woman he will marry. Although he still loves me. It confuses me. Tears at me. I wish I could let go of him without pain, without bitterness. Wish I could carry with me what was special about our love.

The flames have gathered themselves into an amber halo. Across the glow of the fire, across the strait, the outline of the mountaintops has become blurred. Some of the logs are damp and release streamers of smoke that braid themselves into the dusk. I have a sudden image of myself dancing by the fire, weaving around the flames like a ribbon of smoke, threading myself into the texture of the night, alone, dancing cautiously at first, then faster, my feet pounding the sand. I feel out of breath though I haven't left my log next to the fire.

I find myself thinking of the old woman who wears polyester pants and a loose flowered blouse that almost hides her big stomach. Who seems at peace painting the same seascape. Who shares her life with her husband, an old man with slow movements.

And I think of my daughter inside our motel room, turning the glossy pages of her magazine. Surrounded by the old woman's paintings, she sits in the blue chair, her back to the window, scared perhaps because she doesn't look like the models in the pictures. Her face is round, her eyes rimmed with black. I see her less than a year ago, raising her arms to me so I can tuck her in for the night. She smiles. Talks. Her blond hair fans out around her clean face on the pillow.

Suddenly I want to be with her. The shells click in my pockets as I stand up. I hook two fingers into the holes of the reddish stone and carry it pressed against me. It has been warmed by the fire and I feel that warmth through the layers of my clothes, pressing past my ribs and spreading within me.

Other Attics

DOWNSTAIRS THE LANDLADY is cooking pigeons. Steam from her large blue pot moves up the stairs, curling thickly over each step before reaching the next. Under the door of my room it flattens itself and then billows like an overgrown genie, hovering over my bed long before the landlady does.

"Eat," she says. "Eat. It make you strong."

In her country they eat pigeons on Sundays or cook them to nourish the ill. But today isn't Sunday. Thursday maybe. Or even Friday. But not Sunday. And I'm not ill. I can't be ill because I have to get dressed and buy a paper. Help wanted. Always the same question: Reason for leaving previous position? What do they know? All those new beginnings. Why do they stop talking to me after a while? Because I won't cluster whisper with them in the powder room? And the looks. Like the looks of the other landladies.

They all like to poke into my life. They're envious because I don't have to return to rooms cluttered with the voices of husbands and children, envious because I can sleep when I want to. I like to keep myself wrapped in layers of sleep and wait for the geraniums. But this landlady won't let me. She has a round face with gray hair pulled tight across long ears, an eager face with brown eyes and sunken lips where her teeth are missing, an old face that wants to peep into my dream.

"Eat," she says and holds out a thick white plate: mashed potatoes, peas, another one of the small dark bodies like yesterday.

Pale bones show in patches through the soft flesh, bones bleached from boiling. Yesterday she boiled the first pigeon for me. Yesterday I felt dizzy when I touched the floor with my bare feet, nauseous as I took the loose flesh off the bones. Two small mounds: one of dark meat, one of bones; one to flush down the toilet, one to leave on the plate to show my appreciation.

"You like," she said when she came to claim the fragile nest of bones. She looked pleased.

Is there a Slavic delicatessen on an obscure side street where a sad-eyed man with an apron weighs pigeons on a metal scale? Or does the landlady's husband snare them on the roof and keep them in a cage behind the locked door of the potato cellar? Does he fatten them? Talk to them in the gnarled words of his language?

I don't want to know how he kills the pigeons. Does he slit their throats? Snap off their heads? Birdshot would leave pellets in their bodies, pellets that could chip his teeth. The landlady and her husband have few teeth left. He is almost a head shorter than she, a small man with warped shoulders who looks surprised when he sees me on the stairs as though he keeps forgetting he rented me the attic room. On his forehead is a shiny red patch that disappears into his hairline; I wonder if it stops right there or if it continues down the back of his head like a streak.

They live downstairs in small rooms with closed doors. In their living room is a fancy red velvet sofa with plastic covers on the arm rests, a Montgomery Ward TV console, three wooden chairs, a braided rug, and, arranged in front of the sofa and between the chairs, four folding snack tables, grapes painted blue on metal tops. Twice they've invited me into their living room and offered me wrapped pieces of chocolate from a red glass bowl.

Upstairs, my room is large. One open room to fill the attic of the house, one room with slanted ceilings and unpainted floorboards, one room softened by sleep that warms my ankles, my throat, my center. Yesterday I woke to the touch of the landlady's dry fingers against my forehead, to the sound of her voice regretting something I couldn't understand. When I forced my eyes open, she withdrew her large hand and began forming the broken words of her adopted language.

"Doctor," she said, and: "Wait," and: "You no feel good," and: "I make food."

To all this I shook my head, the slow weight of my neck and shoulders pressing against the pillow, the mattress. She has begun to treat me as though I were her child. My own mother has clear words and small hands, hands that don't touch, hands that retreat clasped against her dress. The landlady doesn't have any children; she told me so in long minutes of searching for words and forming substitutes with her hands. Some day I will be an old woman with pale skin on my wrists, maybe a strong, old woman like the landlady who slips one arm behind my shoulders and lifts my head, my neck out of the pillow toward a brown cup that separates my lips and makes me gag on something warm.

"Drink," the landlady says. "Drink. It make you better."

Milk. Warm milk, yes, and something else, almost like honey. I close my eyes and keep my lips warm against the cup tilted, tilted, and then the landlady guides me back into the pillow.

Finally, after she leaves, the geraniums begin to grow by the closet, white geraniums that push their way toward the closet, the door, my bed. If I lie still, they'll form a blanket over me, fragrant, light. A cool blanket. But if I move they will withdraw, pretending they never followed me to this room. Nobody is supposed to see geraniums grow. Ever. Afterwards it's all right to look and notice the growth. But never while they're doing it.

But I am cunning.

I close my eyes and wait. Soon I know the familiar white of the petals against my eyelids, their soft light, and I smile without curving my lips. I know how to. And I can make my breathing shallow. They're beginning to trust me again, moving closer, closer than ever before, until one rigid stem dares to touch my lips, parting them, searching for the moist place under my tongue, and then it stops pushing, stops growing. The geraniums think they are alone; leaves rustle, stems brush against the floor, petals thicken and block the light from my eyelids. When I try to see them through my eyelashes, the landlady is bending over me. The geraniums are hiding, waiting for her to leave.

I won't open my lips. Under my tongue the stem is still hiding. I will keep its secret. But the landlady won't let me. Her large fingers take hold of the end of the stem by my lips, and she pulls, pulls it from my softness and lifts it close to her eyes. In her eyes it becomes a silver stem, and she starts talking rapidly in words I don't recongize.

On the table is a plate with a cooked pigeon. Today's? Yesterday's? How often have I separated flesh from bones? How many more times will have to do it again? I know I must wait until I'm alone. But how can I stop the landlady from rasping up the stairs with yet another offering of her concern? Maybe tonight the geraniums will form a barricade at my door, a barricade that will reach down past the shadows of the stairway and keep the landlady from clutching at my dreams.

"Hospital. Hurry. Very sick." The landlady is speaking into my phone with slow words that come to her in fragments. "Hurry. Sixty-five Helton Road." Children learn to recite their address like that when they're little: Sixty-five Helton Road.

No. Not that. I want to stay. I must get the landlady from my room so she can't let the noise and the cold in. I must push her from my room, my life. Out. Out. She is standing there, watching me. I lift my head to get out of bed, but my shoulders are too heavy; they pull me back. If I rest for a few minutes, I'll be stronger and I'll try again. I close my eyes. But it's no use. The noise begins: humming first, then shrilling, the same noise that has lifted me from other beds, other attics, other houses. Noise that carries me until I'm cold and my legs shiver, until all I remember is that I must not open my eyes to the cold, that I must not tell about the geraniums, even if others probe and touch and shine white lights against the outside of my eyelids again.

Thieves

THE THIEVES EMPTIED the refrigerator and freezer. They took the sirloin steak defrosting next to the sink, a nearly empty bottle of Windex, the green potholders, four bottles from the spice rack, three plastic tankards with see-through bottoms, and the pillowcase from Laura's side of the bed. They did not take the silverware, Phil's new fiberglass tennis racket, the film projector, or the TV set. They left a peculiar combination of emptiness and invasion, a feeling of being smothered and abandoned that clung to Laura's pillow although she changed the sheets and pillow cases right away. It was as though their hands were still on the bed, even after Phil turned off the light and his breathing turned into light snoring that rose and fluttered above him like a kite on a fragile string, lifting and falling with the wind.

Quietly she got up. In the dark she carried her pillow into the living room. Against her bare feet the carpet felt matted, unclean. Tomorrow she would rent a Blue Lustre shampooer at the Taylor Rental Center. She sat down in the stuffed chair facing the front door. Phil had secured it with a piece of yellow rope to keep it closed until the locksmith could come. Returning from the airport where Laura had picked him up from his trip to Seattle, he had first seemed angry when they found their front door forced open, but soon he had settled into amused gratefulness.

"It could have been worse," he had said.

She hadn't answered.

"You're lucky this didn't happen while I was away," he had said.

His relief that they hadn't taken his tennis racket had been painfully obvious to her. Cautiously, with her fingertips, she had touched the things they hadn't taken: her books, her sunglasses, her violin.

At first she hadn't felt anything but a cold tightness at the bottom of her ribs, a surprised chill that grew into anger and spread until she knew she had to do something before it expanded beyond the limits of her body. How she wished she had come upon them stuffing food and spices into her pillowcase. She would have liked to hurt them. Phil would laugh at her thoughts. How important can those potholders and spices possibly be? he'd ask. For Christ's sake, you're pulling everything out of proportion.

The older of the two policemen had said they were going to check the closed camps by the lake. Most of them wouldn't be opened by their owners until the end of June, almost a month from now. Perhaps someone had broken into one of the cottages and needed food. Their house was the nearest year-round residence to those small A-frames that lay abandoned all winter and bustled into ten weeks of frantic activities and bright bathing suits each summer. But why Windex? she had asked. The other officer, a short man with a moustache of various shakes of brown, had shrugged and said it would be worth a try.

Leaving her pillow on the chair, Laura walked back into the bedroom. Falling slanted from the hallway, an oblong block of light covered the foot end of the bed. Phil's snoring, ascending as though he were straining to reach for something above him, dropped and fluttered as he exhaled and then spiraled upward again as if to break the thin kite string. His left arm was flung across the comforter on her side of the bed. She lifted his hand; he flinched but did not wake up. Carefully she set it back down.

For the past eight weeks the bed had been hers. Phil had been away on one of his consulting trips. This afternoon, waiting for him at the airport, she still thought she missed him; but when he walked toward her he wore a beige raincoat she had never seen and looked heavier somehow, paler, as though he had spent most of his time inside offices and restaurants.

She tried to imagine the hands of the thieves, hands that had touched the items she had held so many times, hands that had chosen thyme, garlic powder, dried chives, and paprika. Broad hands with short fingers? Smooth hands with pale skin? Why didn't they select pepper? Cinnamon? Had the thieves been in the middle of preparing a meal and found they were missing several spices? Instead of stopping at the A&P, they had come to her house. Once there, had they emptied her refrigerator and freezer because they decided to finish their shopping trip, much in the manner of someone who stops at the store for a quart of milk and decides, last minute, it might be a good idea to get the weekly shopping over with since the store is so empty? Since there was no bagging service, they must have stuffed everything into her pillowcase: the steak, defrosting for Phil's homecoming dinner, oozing dark blood through the light blue cotton; the open container of cottage cheese, dripping; eggs breaking, running. Why the tankards? Phil had gotten them at a gas station in Holland last fall; they were free with each fill-up. Who would want them? They looked cheap and were uncomfortably light.

She went into the bathroom and took her long robe from the hook on the inside of the door. In the top drawer of Phil's night table she found the flashlight on top of his beige angora socks he kept in there for when his feet got cold at night. It took only seconds to untie the rope that held the front door closed. She left it open and returned into the living room. From the stuffed chair she picked up her pillow and carried it under her left arm, holding the flashlight in her free hand.

Outside, the air was still warm, the humidity lingering from an unreasonably hot May afternoon. Away from her house and the clean scent of freshly cut grass she walked, toward the darkness of the pines that parted to make room for the path she had taken so many times to the lake. The earth felt cool against her bare soles as she stepped into the shadows of the trees. Not once did she stumble. Nearby some small animal scampered into the night.

She could smell the lake, a dank odor of frogskin and milkweed, before she saw its moon-glazed surface. Walking past four of the summer camps, close to each other on quarter acres, she found them looking even more abandoned at night than during the winter.

She turned off the flashlight and pushed it into the right pocket of her robe. Against her bare ankles the damp hem swung heavily. Next to the lake the ground was softer, molding her footsteps and forcing wet particles of soil up between her toes.

She looked at the pillow. Somewhere a bird cried; she didn't recognize its call. Kneeling by the water, she held the pillow in both hands and bent forward. Slowly she lowered it beneath the reflection of the moon until the cold water covered her elbows. Bubbles came up through her fingers. Under her calm hands it moved like a sack of kittens.

Journeys

CASSIE'S MOTHER LIKES to run away from home. She pulls a sun hat over her gray hair, zips Cassie's denim vest over her housedress, and escapes through a window. When Cassie moved her into her house last year, she celebrated her arrival with fresh strawberries and champagne. The following week she called a contractor who replaced the screen doors with ornate gates that bolt into place, but her mother's fierce, tiny body can squeeze itself through any of the downstairs windows.

Usually she heads toward Portsmouth at a brisk pace as if drawn by the ocean where she played as a child; the police have found her wandering along the harbor and in Prescott Park, a few times even on the long stretch of beach next to Wallis Sands. If she returns on her own, she carries scraggly bouquets of weeds and flowers which she pulled up by their roots and which Cassie helps her arrange in empty wine bottles.

Cassie has hired a caretaker for her mother, a young Canadian who studies philosophy at the University of New Hampshire where Cassie works in the infirmary. His name is Chuck, and he is not afraid of the haze of bewilderment that sometimes shifts across the old woman's eyes. He has adjusted his class schedule so he can be with her from three to eleven while Cassie works: he listens to her Beatles records with her, takes her for walks along the Piscataqua River, cooks her favorite dinners, and plays her version of checkers in which she stacks the pieces on five or six squares and moves them in mysterious patterns. Chuck likes to cook and folk dance. His girl friend, Melinda, wears peasant skirts. Both wear Birkenstock sandals and belong to the folklore society in Portsmouth. They go to dances every Saturday and spend weekends at Melinda's apartment.

But during the week Chuck lives in the bedroom where Cassie stores slides and photos of her journeys. When she was in her thirties and forties, she traveled in India and Africa. The longest she stayed in one place abroad was three years when she lived outside Johannesburg and worked with a Belgian doctor who became her lover.

Four times she returned to Africa, to India twice, but for a year now she hasn't traveled at all. Sometimes she tries to imagine the faces of her lovers as they are now, but they come to her in long-ago images, unchanged, some young enough to be her sons. Her own face has changed: her skin is drier; the lines along her eyes and mouth have deepened; her blond hair looks lighter with the silver strands, almost the way it used to get summers when she was a child, bleached by sun and water.

When Cassie was a girl, her mother took her on long trips every year. They traveled through Europe, through Mexico and Japan. Her father owned a company that manufactured light fixtures, and he seldom took even a weekend off. Months before each journey Cassie and her mother would study language and history books. Cassie is certain she inherited her passion for travel from her mother, but now she is the one who has to block her mother's journeys. To keep her from getting lost. From getting hurt. She wishes she had a guide book she could study with her mother to keep her safe, but the books the doctors recommend focus on her disorder as if it were the final destination. She wishes she could keep the doors unlocked and send her mother on her way with the certainty that she'll return unharmed.

Whenever Cassie tells her friends about her mother's latest escape, she laughs. Her friends tell her she is brave to laugh. She doesn't feel brave. Though she is troubled by her mother's periods of disorientation, she can't but laugh at her arriving with a shaggy bunch of flowers, giving her the cautious grin of a child who's been caught doing something forbidden.

Cassie likes to have people over on Saturday evenings for dinner, and her mother decides very quickly if she likes newcomers. "I don't want that person here," she has declared to Cassie on several occasions. Or she might say to a visitor, "You're nice. You can stay." She sits down with everyone for dinner but usually leaves the table halfway through a meal and sneaks into the living room where she takes perfume bottles from handbags which have been left there. In her room she applies splashes of the different scents to her arms and neck before stashing the bottles away. So inventive is she about new hiding places, that it often takes Cassie a week to locate the perfumes and return them to her guests. Old friends have learned to keep their handbags with them.

One summer day, when Cassie unlocks the door to frantic pounding, her mother's wiry body darts past her into the house; a woman almost twice her size and out of breath stops at the bottom of the three steps that lead to the front door. She wears white shorts and new gardening gloves.

"Your mother—," she says, "Your mother keeps taking flowers from my garden."

"I'm sorry."

"I've caught her several times now. I keep telling her . . ."

"I thought she was asleep."

With her left wrist the woman pushes a strand of frosted hair from her damp forehead. "I work hard in my garden."

"I'd be glad to pay—"

"Just make sure she stays out of it."

"I'll drive her past your house and explain to her."

When Cassie gets the woman's address and locks the door, she hears her mother sing the Beatles' "Yellow Submarine" in her room in a thin, high voice. She leans against the wall, closes her eyes and sees herself standing within a blue frame of hours that belongs to her mother, a frame that limits and defines each day, a frame that keeps the journeys she planned in a holding pattern. Taking care of her mother is almost like taking care of a child—except Cassie, who has never given birth, cannot trick herself into the belief that this child will mature, learn, that this is only a phase. What's happening is irreversible. Yet, she feels closer to her mother now than when she was a girl. They laugh more together. Let things go. Her mother used to be a firm parent, a just parent who liked to organize things. Cassie is not nearly as efficient and prefers the lack of structure in their lives. It's as if she were meant to have a child, regardless what age.

She has to knock at her mother's door twice before the singing stops.

"Who is it?"

As if she didn't know. "It's me. Cassie."

"Just a moment." The sound of something moving. Quick, light steps. "Come in, please."

Her mother sits on the wide poster bed, smiling mysteriously, her legs crossed like a skinny Buddha. A waft of clashing perfumes envelops her, and the stolen flowers lie on the windowsill like an offering. The wall hangings and lighter pieces of furniture have been rearranged—the third time this month. She has wrapped rubberbands around her left hand, binding the four fingers just below the knuckles; between the rubber bands and her skin she has secured coins and a blue tissue.

"Here, let me take these. They'll cut off your circulation." Cassie slips the tight rubber bands from her mother's hand. "The woman, the one who followed you—she doesn't want you to take her flowers."

"Oh—" Her mother flips one hand through the air. "That woman."

"How did you get to her house?"

"Well...I had to go."

"Why don't we drive past her house on our way to the store. I'd like to show you where she lives so you won't go there again."

Outside the air is hot. Hot and moist. Cassie's mother carries a basket with a week's accumulation of junk mail which she holds with both hands on her knees as they drive to the development where the woman's house is. They stop in front of the gray colonial with well-tended beds of annuals and perennials. All the houses in the neighborhood are two stories high, painted gray with white shutters or white with gray shutters. Water from buried sprinkler systems covers lawns and shrubs with an even mist. The streets are named after constellations.

Cassie rolls down her window, letting in the heat and rich summer scent of cut grass and flowers. "The woman who followed you lives here. She doesn't want you to take any more flowers from her garden."

Again, her mother flips one hand through the air. "Oh, that woman," she says in the same tone of voice as before, and when Cassie shakes her head and smiles, she laughs aloud.

The air conditioning in the A&P feels like a barrier before Cassie's body adjusts to it. Within the tomatoes and peaches she touches, the cold lies contained like a sleeping wish. Her mother finds a rubber band on the floor and tucks it under the mail in her basket. Voices are hushed as if sucked into the sound system and filtered out with the soft music. Simon and Garfunkel sing "Bridge Over Troubled Waters" and "The Sounds Of Silence" while Cassie's mother sneaks items into the cart which Cassie has to keep removing: Snicker bars, vanilla wafers, red licorice, chocolate syrup. They head for their usual check-out counter where the clerk smiles at them. As the conveyor belt carries fruits and vegetables and bread past her, Cassie's mother sets her basket on

the ground and thrusts her small hands between the groceries. When she can't find the sweets she smuggled into the
cart, she kicks the side of the counter and begins to cry.
Though this happens almost every week, something still
catches at the bottom of Cassie's stomach. She wishes she
could shield her mother from the embarrassment of the
customers in line behind them who stare at the headlines of
the *National Enquirer,* at the floor—any place but at the old
woman whose face is wet with tears.

The check-out clerk winks at Cassie. "How about one of
those nice tangerines, hon?" She takes one from the plastic
bag and extends it to Cassie's mother.

Cassie lays one palm on her mother's arm. "Would you
like to carry the milk?"

Her mother stops with one last dramatic sob. The tan-
gerine in her basket, the gallon jug with the blue label in her
other hand, she precedes Cassie to the car, shoulders thrown
back and head erect as if she'd won a challenge.

The milk is for Chuck, the philosophy student, who goes
through two gallons a week. He unpacks the groceries while
Cassie showers and changes into her white uniform. When
she says goodbye, her mother barely notices her: she is busy
setting up her game of checkers on the kitchen table. Cassie's
schedule is light as usual during summer school, and when
she leaves the infirmary, the moist air has cooled off and feels
like velvet against her neck and arms. She drives with her
windows open. The house is dark, except for the hallway
light which Chuck left on for her.

She looks in on her mother who sleeps curled up on her
right side, one cheek against the mattress, her arms around
her pillow as though it were a stuffed toy. Her lips are
open. On her windowsill stand four wine bottles filled

with bouquets. An old woven blanket hangs over the back of her chair.

Cassie runs one hand across the blanket: it's soft and worn. She carries it into the back yard. Spreads it on the picnic table. The stars look like chips of ice against the dark sky. Lying under the stars, she imagines taking her mother back to the small village in Northern Italy where they bought the blanket from a woman who ran a vineyard. It was the summer Cassie turned twelve, and they were on their way to Rome and stopped for a day in a village high above Lago de Garda. For years her mother talked about returning there, but they never went back.

Cassie sees the stone buildings that cling to the hillside like barnacles when the tide seeps out. *She walks with her mother up the winding road that heaves itself up the mountain. Her mother walks swiftly, blissfully, her arms swinging, her face tilted toward the sun. The air is hot, heavy, and they breathe slowly, aware of each breath. Dust rises under their feet, tinting the landscape the color of the houses and hills—a deep ocher. Most of the houses don't have doors; strands of glass beads cover the open arches. Far below them lies Lago de Garda, its surface a constant blue. The lush green around the shoreline ebbs into hues of browns and reds and yellows that fan from the lake like water bracelets from a pebble.*

On their way down the hill, their path leads them through the vineyard where the woman who sold them the woven blanket all those years ago offers them fresh grape juice and glazed nuts clustered on a stick. Her face is still unlined and brown, her cotton shift the same brick red. She wears a scarf around her hair and invites Cassie and her mother into her house to wash the dust from their faces. When they follow her through the open doorway, luminous beads flicker around them like fragments of stained glass inside a kaleidoscope.

Mushrooms &
Pepperoni & the
Woman in This Story

LET US ASSUME we can see into the mind of the woman who is standing at the sink in the second cottage from the left, looking out of the window above the sink where she is washing the lunch dishes, toward Lake Winnisquan (or any other lake for that matter) past the yellow sign by the road

HI-Vu Cot ages
ousekeeping
Vacancy

a n d

across the road to the small beach where her son is playing right next to the narrow dock which pushes itself into the dark, sluggish water. Holding the fishing rod he borrowed from their neighbor in Connecticut, her husband stands on the dock, paperplatesaresuchawaste, and she remembers the pizza again and the five dollars she puts every week into the harvest-yellow tea pot on the second shelf behindthecups. The woman, we might call her Margaret or, better yet, Beth, doesn't know why lately her mind keeps going over and over her husband's generous gesture last November when, late one Saturday afternoon, he handed her two fives instead of just one for the vacationpot and said (with a smile) that she didn't have to cook that night but could get a large pizza, mushrooms & pepperoni. For over a month it didn't really bother her that she felt thankful and happy while waiting for twenty minutes at the Pizza Palace on North Burlington Street, and that

We will take for granted that Margaret's obsession with the large mushroom & pepperoni pizza is not something she enjoys. Confused by its persistence, she tries to guide her thoughts into a different direction: i should be happy i have a wonderfulhusband and a beautifulhealthychild most of my friends' husbands are not nearly as good to them he is a goodprovider and he doesn't drink or smoke i get the car on tuesdays and fridays and A HOSE CONNECTED TO THE EXHAUST AND LEADING INTO THE WINDOW. Her thoughts are back to visions of suicide. Lately she has been noticing all kinds of things—not that she would ever—reports of suicides in the *Hartford Times,* movies like Hitchcock's *Family Plot,* where the villain is planning a murder disguised as suicide, and Beth lets the water out of the sink. Suicide was a coward's way out of difficulties, everybody knew that, and it was absolutely ridiculous to even think of it as a seductive alternative.

If only she could be as content as her husband. If only her expectations of marriage were as easily defined as his: eggs-andbacon every morning; ironed shirts (light starch on the collar); sex Tuesdays and Fridays, once in a while on Sundays to keep up the 2.4 national average; dinner with his parents in East Hartford every other Saturday. Hers were the preparations and consequences of his expectations: the predictable, greasy cast iron pan, the ironing board in the living room, his refusal to pick up refills of her birth control pills at the pharmacy.

What ever happened to her vague concept of total happiness when she got married? No. We shouldn't laugh. Please. Let's just accept, for the duration of this story, that there are still people who believe in automatic fulfillment through marriage, in princes and dragons and politicians and cold medications and living happily ever after. Margaret is one of those people. But recently she has felt frightened because last November, late one afternoon, she felt happy and thankful for not having to cook, and she stood in line for twenty-five minutes in Mario's Pizzeria on Elm Street, waiting for a large pizza with mushrooms & pepperoni, even though she would have preferred a large pizza with peppers & sausage to a large pizza with mushrooms & pepperoni, which really is beside the point, other than indicating Beth's culinary preferences. And although there most certainly is nothing frightening about a large pizza with mushrooms & pepperoni in itself or, for that matter, any small, medium, or large pizza with any two, three, or four combinations of sausage, anchovies, hamburger, mushrooms, pepper, pepperoni, chocolate syrup, or mozarella cheese, or even a small, medium, or large pizza with everything, we can perhaps understand how gratitude can breed such terror. A SIMPLE GARDEN HOSE. She returns the dishes to the sink and fills it with scalding water.

In twelve days, when they get back home, her husband will begin saving for next year's vacation, perhaps as much as six dollars a week. He talked about it twice on the trip up to New Hampshire, but hasn't quite made up his mind. Beth knows that, come January, he will write for brochures, checking out twenty or thirty places for next summer and, without fail, will decide on the cheapest one. It's amazing how much alike they always are, as if ordered ready-built from a catalog, smelling musty and of canned pine, with thin walls and never too clean, with 40-watt bulbs and cracked linoleum, two blocks from the ocean or, like here, separated by a highway from the lake. Things like that are never mentioned in the brochure. Margaret squirts Ivory from the blue and white bottle and submerges her hands in the lukewarm water.

Tomorrow, as last year and the year before that and before that and before that, they will drive around most of the day and look at those places which, according to her husband, they had almost, almost decided to rent for two weeks, and she never really minded wearing borrowed maternity dresses, and he will find some kind of justification why they didn't get such a bad deal after all, but that next year they will have to be a little more selective, and he will settle down to his vacation, fishing, swimming, eating, saying how nice it is to be away from the office for two whole weeks.

Sitting at his parents' dinner table two months ago, staring past the obedient pot roast into the flame of a narrow white candle

she felt the warmth
rising   into
her elbows and shoulders
to her face   wrapping
her hair into white heat until
the ends
of her hair open
glow   catching
fire small flames hungrily
rushing to her pinkpinkpinkpinkpink
scalp   ahh
warming hugging enclosing sheltering
her glowing burning self
warm patchy-pink-reddened scalp
beautiful frizzled blackened hair
so

He touched her arm: what are you thinking beth father
has asked you twice to pass the mashed potatoes, and, later
in the car when she tried to tell him about it, he smiled: what
you need is anothernother child maybe a little girl thistime
he's almost four you'll see that'll straighten you right out.

For days after getting back to Connecticut she will be
unpacking, washing and cleaning all the items from the list
he made up a month ago and which it took her two days to
crowd into the car: bedsheets, pillows, blankets, dishes,
towels, charcoal (on sale at Bradlee's in Bristol), beach chairs
...her son had to sit between them in front because the back-
seat was too full...pots, flatware, his mother's hibachi, groceries (stores in those vacation areas always charge more),
that fishing pole that their neighbor only reluctantly parted

with. And it will always be like this why am i here with the pillows and blankets which i will take back home and bring to another cottage just like this next summer and take back home again and there will be one more pillow for a-little-girl-this-time and why am i standing standing standing. She has never cooked on a gas stove before. In a cottage as small as this with it TURNED ON AND she pulls her hands from the cold water and withdraws from the image of her head resting sideways in the darkseductive oven.

He waves to her from the dock, and she dries her hands and goes into the bedroom and puts on her purple bathing suit. It makes her legs look white and thinner. Touristlegs. Waiting for some cars to pass so that she can cross the road, Beth wishes she had thrown her sundress over her bathing suit. Bees hover above the bleached picnic table. Her son is making a line of pebbles along the edge of the water, a long parade of Lake Winnisquam pebbles, a slightly curved line from pebbles which he brings out from the lake, wading back and forth, adding to the already existing line of pebbles he is playing with, adding on, making it longer and longer like an endless parade in which enverything and everybody looks alike. Across the sluggish triangle of lead-colored water framed by the dock and beach where her son is lining up pebbles, her husband looks at her over his shoulder and smiles and nothing makes sense will ever make sense again and the bees hang inches above the dark water as though fastened to it like balloons to the child's wrist. They just hang there, lazily, inches above the motionless surface of Lake Winnipesaukee.

Her hands are cold, and the skin around her fingernails is pale and puckered. She watches her son as he wades into the lake, searching for more pebbles. The water covers his ankles, his knees, and then he screams, standing stiffly in the gray water, not moving at all except for his face which is screaming. A bee rises drowsily from his left cheek. Immediately Margaret is by his side, lifting him from the lake, holding him against herself as he howls and begins to struggle in her arms as if he were trying to jump up and down. His wet feet kick against her legs.

"It's all right. Shhh. I'm here. Mommy is here."

"I'll get the first aid spray. Those damn bees." Her husband rushes toward the street.

Bearing her son, she sits down on the coarse, harsh sand. With her right middle finger she takes saliva from her tongue and gently rubs it into the red swelling on her son's cheek. Gradually his screams subside to a whimper as Beth, or Margaret, or even Janice for that matter, rocks her body back and forth, saying over and over: "I'm here. I'm here."

And there is her husband who is so good in emergencies, who got out that green glass bead her son pushed up his nose last year, who deserves a vacation after working so hard for them all year, who is running across the street toward them, waving the first aid spray, and it might not be such a good idea to use the hibachi tonight with all those bees around. She'll fix the hot dogs inside, and maybe tomorrow they'll take their son to Story Land or Animal Forest, he'll like that, and maybe

Tina's Room

I WAKE FROM a dream of holding Tina in my arms, the side of her face warm against my breast, the fierce tug of her lips around my nipple as she draws her nourishment from me. And suddenly I'm afraid I imagined her, imagined the softness of her skin, imagined the circular pattern her hair formed at the crown of her head. I draw my knees close to my body, link my arms around them. My eyes are so dry, they burn.

Andrew stands by the sliding glass door, his back to me, his hands looping his tie into a knot, looking out at the layers of snow that surround our house. Yesterday's sleet has covered everything with a shiny glaze—treacherous perfection. I want to call out for him, but I don't let myself.

This is the image I keep returning to: her narrow back in the terrycloth sleeper, her fingers curled into soft fists next to her head, face turned sideways toward me as I pull the blanket to her shoulders and watch it rising with each breath. An opaque thread of spittle and milk runs from the corner of her mouth to the cribsheet where it will harden into a whitish stain.

But that is afterwards.

And what I need to remember is that last time, those minutes before Tina went to sleep, her eyes open at first, then the sweet heaviness of sleep drawing her lids closed, making them flutter almost imperceptibly before she ceased being awake. Alive.

When did it happen? At what point—exactly—did she cross the line? I continue to feel the stillness, the absolute stillness when I checked in on her an hour later, a stillness that made my legs go numb and made me stop a few steps from her crib before I could move closer and bring myself to touch her.

But that is afterwards.

When nothing can be reversed.

But before—when the blanket still rises with her breaths—I could have lifted her from the crib, could have taken her with me to the living room where often, in the evening, I lay on the sofa, reading or watching TV, letting Tina fall asleep on my stomach, her head resting between my breasts, feeling her become heavier the moment she yielded to sleep. And the rhythm of her breath—always faster than mine. I would have noticed had she stopped breathing. I could have breathed life into her.

Curved and motionless under the negligible weight of the

down comforter, I picture myself outside Tina's room. I raise my hand for the door knob and—

Andrew bends over me. Kisses my temple. "Have a nice day," He says this as if he really wished that for me. His face feels warm and smells of soap, a clean, strong smell which he will carry with him into the winter air. "Getting up soon?" He seems reluctant to leave me.

Of course I tell him, "Soon," but I don't think he believes me. What else can I do? I can't talk with him about Tina. Or about her death though the doctors gave me labels of absolution: crib death, sudden infant death. *There's nothing you could have done to prevent it.* Yet, for five months I've left her room untouched, have left her memory untouched with words. Her door is closed.

Sometimes I stay in bed all day. There, it is safe to imagine myself outside Tina's room, my hand on the door knob. There, I can even turn the knob. She is still asleep, her fingers curled into soft fists next to her head—

No, not that one.

I want the one where she's awake. Her eyes are open, and in the light of the July afternoon, her fine hair shimmers in a circular pattern at the crown of her head. We've given her my grandmother's name—Christina Anne—but we call her Tina. She reaches for me, and I bend over her. As I lift her into my arms, she rests her warm face in the hollow on the side of my neck right above my collar bone...

I can make this last.

All day, if I'm careful not to let anything else in.

I can be with her.

Hold her.

Make her disappear before Andrew gets home in the evening.

My stomach growls, and I cover it with my hands. My belly is flat, empty. When we moved into this house, it was stretched tight. I was in my last month of carrying Tina and assured of her life by the sudden movements within me.

Sudden.

Sudden infant death.

Crib death.

Where the crib becomes the open coffin. And all that remains is a whitish, oblong stain of hardened spittle and of milk she sucked from my breasts and which I saw trickling from her mouth. Movement. Her breath rising. My hand pulling the blanket to her shoulders, smoothing it. A sequence of movements and then stillness.

And what Andrew finds hard to forgive—I believe—is that I was the last to witness her movements, the first to witness her stillness.

I would like to be able to lay the blame on something, to be able to say: she died *because*—

But there is no cause. No reason that can make sense. And so we are silent with each other though, sometimes, I wonder if Andrew, too, has an image he keeps returning to, a comforting image, perhaps, of holding her in his arms, one of his hands supporting her head, the lamp by his chair illuminating her fair hair, her fingers curled around his thumb—

But perhaps I imagined all that—Andrew holding her, bending over her ... the pattern of light on her hair ...

her warm infant smell of milk and sleep as I lift her from her crib—

I press my eyes closed, try to evoke her, touch her. My legs feel cold. My entire body does. I'm a cold weight against the mattress. Sinking deeper. Away. The last moment I remember of being fully alive is when I pulled the blanket to Tina's shoulders. I cannot imagine ever having another child. This, I believe, is something else Andrew cannot forgive.

What I want is to wrap myself into the lightness of holding Tina, of staying here in bed with her all day. I tear at my memories, try to force them into surrendering the familiar shape of my child. But she won't come to me. She won't. Everything feels flat. Artificial. The reality of not having a child has become stronger than any image of her I can evoke.

Some day, I knew, I would have to enter her room—really enter it—but I didn't know when, didn't think it would be this soon. It's safer in my fantasies to enter. Much safer. Because then I can have Tina with me, inside her room, inside her crib by the window where I left her that afternoon five months ago.

But what if I did imagine her? Imagined a child. Imagined a death. A death to explain to myself why I don't have a child.

Outside her door I stop, my hand on the knob. That's how it always goes in my fantasies. But this time is different. A cool draft shifts around my bare legs, and I draw my bathrobe closer around myself. On the wooden floor, my feet feel brittle. Inside that room is a stillness that might wrap itself around me, swallow me the moment I open the door.

Dust lies on her dresser, on the pleated shade of the lamp; it mutes the green of the carpet and rises under my feet as I walk toward the window where her crib stands. The mattress is bare: shiny plastic with clown faces. Grinning clown faces with red circles for cheeks. I wish I could hear the sounds of small children playing in the street, but it is silent out there. Only the dark shapes of squirrels hush across the smooth surface of the snow with quick, twitchy movements, their tails jerking upright. One sits on the birdfeeder, head stretched forward, its reddish fur tinged with gray. Light seeps through its frayed tail. The rodent mouth opens and closes rapidly, emitting hoarse sounds that are somewhere between a bark and the cry of a child.

Sharply, I rap against the window, and the hurried claws scatter for safety. It jumps off—in a wide arc—as if trying to fly, and skids across the glazed snow toward the birches.

Carefully, I open the drawers of the dresser I painted and stenciled for her. Dresses, stretch suits, socks—she would have outgrown them by now. I run my hands across the undershirts that weren't washed often enough to yellow. *Tina?* They still carry a faint scent of the lotion I used to rub on her smooth skin after her bath.

I close my eyes against the tears, but then I let them. I take in a deep breath and slowly begin to see myself packing her things into the boxes the movers left here last spring. Pack them, and then give them to Goodwill. Keep the door to her room open—at least a gap. Give away the crib, the dresser, the lamp I bought the day I found out I was pregnant. Andrew and I were in Montreal that week. He celebrated by ordering a bottle of champagne; I celebrated by buying the first item for our child's room: a wicker lamp with a pleated shade.

I lift thin cotton blankets from her drawers. Pile them on top of the dresser with her clothes. Narrow stacks of pale colors. Two crib sheets, both white with blue ducks. I remember pulling them over the plastic of the mattress, across the smiling clown faces, remember their tight fit, remember how I gently lowered my daughter onto the sheet.

Yes, that was real.

As real as finding her without movement.

As real as standing now in her room, searching for the plain yellow sheet, the one Tina died on. Someone—I don't know who—took off the crib sheet, and I try to remember if it was in that first load of wash I did after her death. I pull out her last pieces of clothing, her towels, and there it is—the sheet— wedged in back of the bottom drawer, folded into a square so tight and small that, at first, it looks like a washcloth.

If I want to, I can close my hands around it—that's how small it is.

If I want to, I can pretend it doesn't exist.

It feels dry and smooth as I unfold it. The stain is gone. As though it had never happened. But it did happen. We had her with us for two months and 26 days. We gave her my grandmother's name—Christina Anne—but we called her Tina. I lift the sheet against the window and hold it there, hold it until—in the winter light—it moves as if caught by a breath and relinquishes the outline of a sleeping child.

Where Are You Going?

"WHERE ARE YOU going, Jessamyn?"

Two months ago Walter began reading my horoscope. I'm an Aries. Impatient, enthusiastic, generous, moody, energetic, inconsiderate, Walter tells me. I wouldn't know; I don't believe in horoscopes: I like to be in control of my own life. According to Walter, I am about to go on a journey, a long journey. Watching me closely for my reaction, he reminds me that almost every week my horoscope has something about a long journey in it.

"Where are you going?"

"Nowhere." I stroke the back of my Persian cat.

"Don't think you can hide this from me, Jessamyn."

On the table in front of him the evening paper is opened to the page with the horoscopes. We have lived in this house for the four years of our marriage, and we don't have doors for the bedrooms yet. The tiles for the kitchen floor are still stacked in the garage; the porcelain lamp for the dining room remains packed in the attic; one single light bulb sways above the table. Walter is a man of elaborate preparations. But he never gets beyond them. We live in a house filled with unfinished projects, projects that lose their importance as Walter moves on to something new. This time my horoscope. I wonder when he will abandon it.

For a man of thirty-one Walter looks older than he is. His light brown hair is thinning; he combs it sideways to cover the top of his head. Sometimes I wonder why I married him. Sometimes he bores me. Yet, in a way, I find it reassuring to know what it is about him that will continue to bore me. Maybe it has to do with expectations. I'm not sure. With not expecting too much. Walter is a successful man. He works in advertising, writing slogans that sell cereals, soaps, cars, cosmetics, appliances, dog food.

His obsession with my horoscope is the most interesting recent development in our marriage. The things that used to interest both of us have stopped. Fizzled out. Kaput. We met playing tennis, played two or three times a week until we married. Then it went down to once a week—an amazing parallel to our sex life—until Walter developed tennis elbow and we stopped altogether. With tennis, that is. The sex hasn't stopped entirely. Not yet. But if I were to draw a curve, there is only one way it would go: Down.

"Where are you going?"

I have begun to wait for the evening paper. At four-thirty it is delivered, one hour before Walter gets home. If I read my horoscope before he does, I can predict part of our evening: *be careful with money matters* has him check the balance in our account; *keep to routine matters early in the day* makes him suggest my chores for the next morning; *don't waste time with an insincere friend* starts him on a lengthy discussion on friends, acquaintances, neighbors; *good news travels slowly* has him ask if I got any mail; *a new romance on the horizon* makes him suspicious of other men.

"Are you ever attracted to other men, Jessamyn?"

Attracted. A strange word. Moths are attracted to light. *Burn.* Against their will. Out of control. I would feel uncomfortable being out of control.

"No, Walter. I am not attracted to other men. Are you?"

"To other men?"

"No. Women."

"Of course not."

Walter is faithful. He has told me so. For three reasons he is faithful:

1. he does not want to catch a disease;
2. he does not want to get another woman pregnant;
3. he does not want another woman to fall in love with him and follow him home.

I believe Walter is faithful because he does not like sex.

Attracted. I have begun to look at other men to figure out what attraction means. Last week I found myself staring at the man who works in the bookstore, wondering if his black beard was soft or coarse, what it would feel like against my palm should I cup my right hand around the side of his face and bring it close to mine ...

No, Walter. I am not attracted to other men. I would not call it attraction. Lust, perhaps. Imaginary lust. Imaginary, controlled lust. In my fantasies I am caressed, desired, thinner. Always thinner. And if my fantasies don't work for me, I revise them, changing bodies, situations, dialogue, my self-image. Never faces. My imaginary lovers are faceless. They never reject me. They do not comb their hair sideways; they do not date the bottoms of Kleenex boxes to keep track of how long they last; they do not turn their back toward me at night; they are not interested in my horoscope, even if it says: *You are about to embark on a long journey. Prepare well.*

"Where are you going, Jessamyn?"

Certainly not to the strawberry bed. Two years ago Walter planted a strawberry patch behind the house, planted it and never set foot in it again. I am the one who has stooped to weed, who has gathered them. Walter likes to eat strawberries: he dips them into sour cream, then brown sugar. Walter also likes to give me advice on how to care for his strawberry patch, and he tells the neighbors how hard he works in it. Never again shall I enter Walter's strawberry bed. He doesn't know yet; it is still too early in the spring.

This morning I taught kindergarten. I'm a substitute teacher; the elementary school calls me in two or three times a week. Just before recess I overheard two girls, talking by the window. One of them said: "When people suffocate, they turn invisible whenever they get close to the color brown." The other nodded, seriously, totally accepting the bizarre statement. To me it makes as much sense as Walter's question. Is he trying to sell me on the idea of leaving? Or is he afraid I might leave?

Does it matter?

"Where are you going?" Walter is observing me, two narrow lines vertical on his forehead.

My father used to frown at me like that when I didn't listen to him, when I didn't obey immediately. He would frown, and then he would begin to count, slowly: One, two, two-and-a-half, two-and-three-quarters, two-and ... Never higher than that; by two-and-a-half I was usually running, certain that, if he ever got to three, something terrible would happen.

I never found out.

I never waited long enough.

Are you counting too, Walter?

Waiting for me to run?

Run where?

Perhaps back to the bookstore. I have since spoken to the man with the black beard. His voice is soft; I still don't know about his beard. We went for coffee across the street and talked about Tolstoi. When he said it is acceptable to read new books—books untested by time—in paperback, but a sin to read Tolstoi in any other form than leather-bound, I pictured thick, red leather volumes, gold-tooled with Tolstoi's initials. A snob, I thought, a bloody, intellectual snob. Yet, I would like to speak with him again, to find out how he reads Faulkner, Woolf, Kafka, to find out the texture of his beard.

"When are you going?"

"When?" Under my hand the cat stretches. Purrs. A sound like a finely tuned mechanism.

"No, Jessamyn. I asked: Where?"

"I heard you say: When are you going?"

"You misunderstood. I asked: Where are you going?"

The more Walter talks about the journey, the more plausible it becomes that I could go away.

Might go away.

Might want to go away.

Not that I'm planning to leave, but if I did, I would not choose a one week excursion-fare-special to some tropical island. Postcard palms against a sunset sky. Natives dancing. Complimentary cocktail and airport transfers included. Not for me. Not that. It would have to be a long journey. A journey to a place already prepared for me, waiting for me. Two large rooms with high ceilings. A window seat. Walls painted ivory. Shelves filled with books and plants. Woven rugs and pillows. My piano. A low bed on a white platform. Batiked covers in shades of blue.

But where?

Not another secluded country house for me. A city. I would live in a city on the top floor of an old stone building. Close to museums, theatres, concerts. A city where I have not been before. San Francisco, perhaps. Steep sidewalks: paved. I'd see the bay from my bedroom window, listen to my Brahms records at night, work days at a school teaching the children of other women. I almost had a child once. But it bled from me in the third month.

You are about to embark on a long journey. Prepare well.

I know a woman by the name of Pat who left her husband.

I also know Margot, Sandy, Mary.

Lots of others.

Women with children.

Women without children.

If I had children, I would give them names like Anne or Bob or Jane or Ted. Easy names. Names that would not get in their way. Names that would not draw attention like mine: Jessamyn. When strangers hear my name, they form the wrong image. Walter first heard my name from a friend and asked to meet me because he fell in love with my name. Jessamyn. Jessamine. Jasmine: an ornamental plant with fragrant white blossoms.

Misleading.

Walter, I am not ornamental. Nor am I fragile.

I think of myself as Jess. My parents called me Jess. But Walter likes to listen to the sound of the word Jessamyn as he says it.

Would it be easier to leave if I had children to take with me? Or would it be harder, knowing I needed to *prepare well* for anyone other than myself? My cat I would take with me, that I know, although I still haven't found the right name for her. I know the texture of her fur, know the sound that begins deep within her throat. But not her name. Not yet.

"When are you going, Jessamyn?" Walter is waiting.

This time I heard him clearly. He did ask: When?

Why have I stayed until now? Do I find it comforting to predict what I will be bored by tonight? Tomorrow? Or do I only think of leaving Walter when the time is not right? Like self-examining my breasts. I know I should do it once a month. But I don't because I only think of it when I'm fully dressed and not alone.

How to know when the right time has come to leave?

Is there ever a right time?

When did all those other women decide to leave? When it became unbearable for them to stay for one more day? Or when they could not name one more reason for staying?

When am I leaving, Walter?

Soon, I think.

Soon.

Night Voices

AND HE ALWAYS falls asleep before I do. Can I get you any-thing? he asks before he turns on his right side, before his breathing becomes slower. Can I get you anything? What do I need? A clean sheet cool against my legs, I lie on my back in Carla's bed. She'll always be fifteen, never changing, her face smiling as the morning she left for school, the morn-ing of the accident. Emily gets older, forty-two last May; even her children are older than Carla was, will be. Yet, I feel closer to my dead daughter, to my

Night after night in the narrow beds of our daughters. Sleep in the front room, she tells me. Go ahead. Sleep in the big bed by yourself if that's what you want. How can I leave her alone in the back room at night? I feel her body across the room, silent, reproachful. Before I turn to the wall, I ask if I can get her anything.

first child. Through the screen the birches stand white against the pines, their crowns swallowed by dark. Crickets I hear, but no sounds of traffic. He'd rather sleep in the front room with the street noise, sleep in the big bed. That was fine when the girls were small, when I was tired at the end of the day. Then the sounds of cars never bothered me: there were less; still, I never minded them. Now I

Shelves for the basement. Paint the porch and the garage. Buy boards to build a birdfeeder. I'll mount it in the kitchen window. She can watch the birds if the mailman is late. Bluejays we get. Sometimes a cardinal.

never get tired; there's not enough to do to get tired; not even making breakfast. He gets up first and I can hear him in the kitchen: the refrigerator when he gets the eggs, butter hissing in the pan, the toaster. Let me, he says, you've done for so many years. Did I ever complain? One slice

Catalog the slides. I keep busy. Letters from Emily and the grand-children. That's all she cares about. Letters and Sunday phone calls. Emily hasn't written for two months; short letters, one sentence for each grandchild: Kevin likes his job. Audrey is saving for a car. We call them Sunday afternoons. In case they sleep late.

of toast I used to eat, sometimes a small piece of sharp white cheese; no more than that. Now I must eat warm yellow eggs to please him, to give him something to get up for in the morning. So much time to fill restlessly. I keep busy, he tells Emily; and: How's everything? he asks, watching me move the warm yellow eggs from the fork into my mouth, watching. How's everything? This used to be

Paint the porch and the garage. Shelves for the basement. Buy boards.

Carla's bed; he sleeps in Emily's, closer to the door. Sometimes he mumbles in his sleep, mumbles words that thicken before I can understand. Only the tone of his voice changes, becomes urgent or pleading, fades into silence, and then all I hear is his breathing, still as strong as when he was young and fell asleep with my left arm under his neck, one of his knees

thrown across my thighs. Thousands of hours I have listened to him breathe until the color of the sky begins to change to softer shades of slate; thousands of hours I have watched the birches pressing

through the dark, pressing against the house, lifting their branches from the sky as if by sheer will; thousands of hours I have watched over his breath until

I too may sleep. I cannot ask him if his chest hurts or if he took the small pills after dinner. Strong he likes to feel, strong and

busy, even if it means taking my work from me or painting the house every

Her shallow hours of sleep in the early morning. Let me hold you, I tell her many nights. Let me hold you. She says: I'll only keep you up. Gray, smooth, her hair lies on the white pillow. Her face thinner. Thinner all the time. Emily hasn't written for two months. Carla's favorite color was blue. Today I'll buy the boards to build a feeder. She can watch the birds if the mailman is late. Sometimes he doesn't come until eleven. Thinner all the time. I make her breakfast. Scramble fresh eggs. Butter two slices of toast for her. Set the kitchen table with her good china. So many years she rushed to get breakfast for me early. Now she can start the day leisurely. For special occasions she saved the good china. I make sure she eats. Eats well. Ten in the morning she starts waiting by the window. Bluejays we get. Sometimes a cardinal.

Marya

CURVED IN THE warmth of Kevin's embrace, I hear his wife, Marya, in the room across the hall—that familiar whimper, like a kitten almost, she makes in her sleep just before she wakes up. I press my palms against my ears. Crawl deeper into the nest of our bodies to make myself small.

Smaller.

Still, I hear everything. Even Kevin's breath which is deep. Measured. He breathes the way he thinks. Some nights it's harder than others to get up for Marya, especially when I'm still moist between my thighs and don't like going into her room smelling of him. But if I don't, Kevin will have to get up, and that would be worse. Not that he doesn't offer—but he looks relieved when I feed her, clean her, brush her pale wisps of hair.

Kevin is brilliant. A partner at Davidson and Whorley. Always kind. That's what I liked best about him from the beginning—his kindness. One of the other secretaries told me about Marya three days after I started working there. Brain tumor. Most men would send a woman like Marya to a nursing home, but Kevin believes it's important for her and the children to be together. James is four, Pammy two. Soon after her birth the tumor was discovered.

Late in the afternoons, when I get home from the office and the nurse leaves, I carry Marya into the living room and prop her into the recliner with three pillows on each side to keep her from tipping out. I let her hold Pammy in her arms, but I kneel next to her to make sure her daughter won't slip from her. Pammy resembles her mother. In a healthy way. Just the coloring. Blond hair and blue eyes. The way I always wanted to look.

James likes to feed his mother. He has told his grand-parents that he has an Elizabeth and a Mommy. "An Elizabeth," he said, "takes care of you, but you take care of a Mommy."

Marya's whimpering has faded. She must be awake now, uncomfortable, perhaps even afraid though I make sure to leave on the night light for her when I tuck her in at night. I bought it for her the day after I moved in, hoping the light would give her peace at night. It's in the shape of Popeye. Not that I like it, but it was the only night light in the store.

I could wait for Marya to fall back asleep, but her silence draws me toward her room more strongly than any sound she might make. Some day, I know, that silence will remain, but until then it's only a deceptive sign of release.

Hers.
Mine.

I picture her head raised on two pillows, patches of hair clinging to her skull, eyes flat within the sharpened features that barely hide the death she nurtures within her. None of the caring goes to her—she diverts it, assigns it to the death shape that is molding her around its image. Before her illness she was lovely. I've seen her photos in the leather albums. Long blond hair. A determined look about her. Yet, if I look closely at those pictures, I can already see it, that death shape she carries within her. With some people you can. My brother, Al, was one of them. Although he wasn't ill. Just spiteful, and it was I who wished the death for him. He was twelve, a year older than I, and though it was his choice to ride my father's motorcycle that night, though I was asleep when the death shape took him over, I'd seen it waiting within him for a long time.

If you wish for something strongly enough, you can bring it on. But only if you believe that you can.

Careful not to disturb Kevin, I disengage myself from his arms, slide out of bed, and cover myself with the sweatshirt robe his children gave me for Christmas. Kevin bought it, of course, but James picked it out. It's bright red. Kevin likes to give me presents—a single rose or a bunch of perfect grapes. Little things, some might say, but to me they show that he thinks of me and tries to find ways to please me.

Outside Marya's room I stop. The floor is cold, and from below my feet comes the slow rumbling of the furnace. I take a deep breath, but it still chokes me as I open the door, that adult smell of feces—so much harder to bear than that of an infant. Though Marya too wears diapers. Though Marya, too, is helpless. Except with her it's in a reverse kind of way. With an infant you see signs of change, improvements as the baby becomes stronger and more capable. With Marya the changes are all a decrease: control, movement, recognition. At times I wonder how much she understands.

Popeye casts his bluish glow on Marya's face. Her shallow eyes look through me as I clean her buttocks with the scented tissues I pluck from the plastic box with the photo of the smiling baby in front. Marya only weighs 87 pounds, eleven less than when I moved in here the end of last summer. As I lift her, I try not to think of dead weight though that's what it feels like—sagging bones and skin. She is a tall woman. When I imagine Kevin doing this for her all through last year, touching her, raising her shoulders to fluff up the pillows, perhaps holding her to comfort her—

It's not that I often think of them together. But it has to be harder for him than for me.

Marya's parents come to visit her every Saturday afternoon at three and sit on both sides of the recliner in the living room. They're blond and large-boned and healthy. Between them, Marya fades even more. Recedes into the white cotton blanket I spread across the recliner to keep her skin from sticking to the vinyl. Her parents—they too look through me. As if I were the one who'd caused her to be like that. As if I'd taken Kevin away from her. But he'd already parted from her long before I arrived, only keeping his vigil by her side.

Marya closes her eyes. Her lids are rice-paper thin. Carefully, I brush a strand of damp hair from her forehead and step back from her bed. On my toes I walk to the door and pull it gently shut behind me, leaving her resting in the blue light. In the bathroom I wash Marya's smell from my hands. The children's rooms are at the end of the hall. First I check on Pammy. She lies on her stomach, elbows tucked close to her sides. Like a small animal, I can't help thinking as I smooth the blanket up over her shoulders. James sleeps on his back, a frown on his face as though he were trying to resolve something. Both are still young enough to start calling me *Mother* after Marya is gone, perhaps even to remember me as their mother once they're grown.

Kevin has turned over when I return to bed, and I slip into my space under his blanket, trying to gather warmth from the length of his back. I think of him and Marya and the children, before I came to live here, the four of them, asleep during a night like this, vulnerable without anyone watching over them.

My breath takes up the pattern of Kevin's, slow and steady, and I picture another night, almost like this, a few weeks or months from now, a night when I'll wake up to the sound of an unfamiliar silence from Marya's room. I'll lie here without moving, testing the silence to see if it will remain, a silence which—until that night—can only be a deceptive sign of release.

Breaking the Rules

I HATED ST. THERESA'S from the first day I saw the U-shaped brick building with the white columns, walked through the tiled hallways that echoed my steps, and sat at one of the long tables, presided over by a stern faced nun who admonished me for touching the tablecloth with my elbows. The room I shared with three other girls was painted stark white, and we were forbidden to hang any pictures on the walls, except on the corkboards above our beds. One of many rules—yet one of the few that made sense: if we left nails in the walls, there'd be evidence we'd lived here. The nuns wanted to file us through, replicas of each other in blue pleated skirts and white blouses, and then have us exit without leaving a trace.

What I hated most was that we had to call them *Mother*. Mother Monica, Mother Elizabeth, Mother Catherine,

Mother Barbara... I was not about to call a swarm of black-robed strangers *Mother.* My mother was an opera singer who often was away from home for weeks at a time. I didn't know my father; he lived in Italy where my mother had studied voice for two years before returning pregnant to New York. She'd never kept it a secret from me that she'd wanted a child without, as she called it, "the confinement of marriage." Though at times I wished for a live-in father, I felt special knowing she had chosen me, and I liked not having to share her with anyone when she was home.

A few years ago a magazine had published an article about my mother with a photo of her and me: *we're both wearing white blouses with lace collars and long black skirts; my mother's left hand rests lightly on my shoulder; we sit on the piano bench, our profiles turned to the photographer, and I hold on to my reserved, yet dignified, smile that I've practiced in front of the mirror, a smile I believe matches hers, but which in the photo looks totally different from the expression on her face, which is one of having gathered herself deep inside, an expression of contentment I can't possibly hope to match.* The reporter had written that my father had died when I was an infant.

"To protect you," my mother had told me. "Some people wouldn't understand. It's enough if you and I know."

Mrs. McQuarrie knew too. She was our housekeeper and looked after me when my mother was on tour. Fourteen years ago, when I was born, she'd come to live with us. While my mother's appearance changed depending on clothes and hairstyles, Mrs. McQuarrie, who now was a head shorter than I, reassuringly stayed the same in her huge seersucker housedresses and the size six white orthopedic shoes. Every couple of months she gave herself a permanent which tightened her gray hair and drew it close against her scalp. When my mother was away, Mrs. McQuarrie and I read romance novels which she bought at Kresgie's drug store. Each paperback cover showed a beautiful woman in a long gown fleeing from a mansion, and the books always ended with the woman's marriage to the man she'd fled from.

It was in one of those romances that I'd first come across the word illegitimate. One of the characters, a villain who tried to swindle the hero out of his inheritance, was illegitimate. I'd looked it up in my dictionary, and it meant: born out of wedlock ... unlawful ... incorrect. I didn't like the word; there was nothing unlawful or incorrect about my mother having me.

I don't think it was because of the romances that my mother decided the company of Mrs. McQuarrie wasn't enough for me, but shortly after my fourteenth birthday she began talking about "intellectual stimulation ... the proper environment...," and though I protested, I was shipped off to boarding school in Connecticut on September 5, 1962.

Since I didn't want to call the nuns *Mother,* I avoided any form of direct address. *Hey you* was out of the question; we were considered young ladies and critically observed for any slip of manners. *Excuse me* worked most of the time.

"Excuse me, I'd like to mail this letter."

"Excuse me, may I be excused?"

I wondered what the nuns' hair looked like under their habits. All chopped off? Tied back? Did they keep it covered even at night? What did they do behind those doors that were off-limit to us? Though they sat with us during meals, we never saw them eat. Their faces were pink, dry, and the powdery smell of starch followed them everywhere. When they walked along the halls, they kept their arms crossed in front of them, hands hidden inside their wide sleeves. Like magicians they were able to produce an uncanny array from those sleeves: pencils, prayer books, eyeglasses, crumpled tissues.

Every morning in church they kneeled in the two front rows, their faces lifted toward the altar and the young chaplain. The name of God had a way of surfacing whenever they talked, whether it was in a biology lecture, during a conversation about the meatloaf, or while dissecting an Emily Dickinson poem. It gave them a peculiar logic of their own—everything could be explained and justified by bringing in God as the cause.

It seemed every five minutes a bell rang to indicate where we should be: at the chapel, in the classroom, on the playground, in the dining hall...A bell when to study, eat, brush our teeth. And each bell, each rule, became a challenge. It didn't make sense to arrange my bedspread just one certain way, to line up my shoes in back of the closet, to fold my underwear and towels so they were stacked like books. I didn't like someone watching how I held my fork, or how much I ate, or how straight my back was when we lined up for the weekly inspections of our uniforms on Friday evenings.

How I missed the afternoons when I'd sat with Mrs. McQuarrie in our kitchen, elbows propped on the table, eating warm apple pie with slabs of cheddar cheese until my stomach felt taut. When my mother was home, she ate sparingly: "So I won't become one of those fat sopranos."

I liked having a mother who was famous. People recognized her in restaurants and stores and asked for her autograph. Occasionally I saw her picture in papers or magazines, her pale face emerging from her cloud of black hair like an unexpected gift. Whenever she performed in New York, she reserved first row orchestra seats for Mrs. McQuarrie and me. Opening night I'd sit there in my best dress, listening to her strong, clear voice, pretending to myself that she was singing for me alone. She looked so lovely up there on stage, moved with such grace, that— sometimes—I forgot to breathe.

If she took me along to a party afterwards, I'd stay next to her all evening, watching her smile when people said how much I resembled her. The summer I turned twelve, I traveled with her to San Francisco where she sang the lead in *Aida,* and I watched the rehearsals from the wings. We had a suite with a grand piano on the eighteenth floor of the Mark Hopkins. The first time we ate in the dining room, a girl about my age sat at the table next to ours with her parents, who argued throughout the meal. Silently, the girl sat between them, staring at her plate. Once, when she glanced up and saw me watching her parents, her face turned a bright red, and she quickly looked away. I was glad I only had one parent.

Our third evening in San Francisco I started feeling sick, and when my mother took my temperature, it was up to 102. She was wearing her long blue gown, ready to leave for a reception given in her honor. One of the maids offered to stay with me, but my mother made a phone call and then changed into her bathrobe.

"I'd rather be with you than with anyone else," she said and ordered a large pitcher of apple juice from room service; we talked until I fell asleep.

Why then would she send me to boarding school—if it really was true what she'd said about rather being with me than with anyone else?

"Don't you think I'll miss you too?" she said when I asked her that the day she took me to St. Theresa's.

"If you did, you wouldn't leave me here."

We didn't have much time together that day because the nuns kept making a fuss over her, almost as much of a fuss as they made over the young blond chaplain who taught religion and had a permanently bewildered smile on his round face, and who seemed incapable of maintaining the discipline in his classes that appeared a natural to the nuns. He probably was too embarrassed to admit to the nuns that he couldn't control us, and he kept trying to ignore the caricatures of him which we passed around. As soon as he turned to write something on the chalkboard, we'd start humming: "It was her itsy bitsy teeny weeny yellow polka dot bikini…"

Friday evenings, when we assembled in the auditorium, nuns with clipboards walked along our rows, looked us up and down, and noted demerits for everything that wasn't according to regulations. Poor posture meant one demerit; a torn shoelace two demerits; unkempt hair one demerit; a spot on a skirt or blouse three demerits … A total of ten demerits or more meant having to stay on weekends, the only time we were permitted to leave St. Theresa's. My first week I accumulated twenty-seven points and had to spend Saturday rearranging my closet and writing my number—137—inside my books.

Mother Monica, a gaunt nun with facial hair, was in charge of censoring. Of the sixty-two books I'd packed, only thirty-eight were returned to me with her initials *MM* in the upper right hand corner of the first page; the others were held in her office until my mother could take them home. I got to keep Mark Twain and the Bronte sisters, my Dostoyevsky set, of my Hemingways only *The Old Man And The Sea*. The rest, according to Mother Monica, were too mature for me. Even my Agatha Christies were confiscated, along with Hawthorne's *The Scarlet Letter* and Salinger's *Franny And Zooey* which my best friend, Jocelynn, had given to me as a good-bye present. To be caught with a book that didn't carry Mother Monica's initials cost five demerits.

I was sure none of Mrs. McQuarrie's romances would have earned the *MM* of approval.

137—that number had to identify everything I owned: clothing, school supplies, washcloths, toothpaste ... Until that first Saturday, when Mother Irene made me empty my closet and gave me her laundry pen, I'd avoided marking any of my belongings; after all—I wouldn't be here for long; soon, my mother would let me come home. But that Saturday, sitting alone on my bed while my roommates were visiting their families, I wrote the number 137 on the labels inside my skirts, my blouses, my underwear, and with each smudged stroke of the black ink I felt further away from my mother.

She called that evening, told me she missed me, but I didn't believe her.

"Then why did you send me away?"

For a moment she was silent. "It's an excellent school. I wish—"

"But I hate it here."

"You're not giving it a chance."

It frightened me that anyone, even my mother, should hold that kind of power over me, the power to keep me in a place where I didn't want to be. She had chosen to have me. What had changed?

She told me she'd mailed a package to me two days ago, but when I got it, the nuns had marked a large 137 next to my name. Though the letter inside ended: *Love, Mother,* I knew most of the contents had been chosen by Mrs. McQuarrie: her coconut macaroons and soft poundcake with raisins; marzipan loaves coated with chocolate from the Bremen House on Eighty-sixth Street; smoked almonds, and those triangles of Austrian cheese she knew I liked. My mother had included light blue stationery, a camera, and three rolls of film. Did she really think I wanted to take pictures of anything here?

Everyone's packages were kept inside a windowless room with wide shelves next to the study hall and released to us for one hour on Monday and Thursday afternoons, when we'd gorge as much as we could before they would be locked away again. To be caught with food from home at any other time brought five demerits. Dinners on Mondays and Thursdays were frugal: the nuns counted on us not wanting to eat much after those afternoon binges.

After the Friday inspection a bell would ring, and we'd take seats in the auditorium—silently, because to whisper meant another demerit—and then the Mother Superior, a heavy nun with black eyebrows and long teeth, would mount the stairs on the side of the stage, her black skirts brushing the waxed floor boards, and position herself behind the lectern. Mournfully, her eyes would sweep over us before she reached for her bifocals and read the names of those girls who had more than ten demerits. Since she started with the highest number, my name frequently was among the first on her list. After a brief hesitation she launched into the speech which I came to recognize and expect, right down to the meaningful pauses, the mournful glances, the words which prompted her to reach for her bifocals.

"It worries me," she'd start, "that there are still some of you who don't appreciate the special opportunity you've been given, who still are disorderly, undisciplined, and without the proper respect. I know many girls on the outside who would give anything—" A meaningful pause, "anything to be here, whose names are on a long waiting list. And it breaks my heart to tell them we don't have room for them ... *Yet*—" Here her voice would break abruptly as though she were choking on her pity for those unfortunate girls on the outside, and she'd remove her bifocals and execute another mournful sweep with her eyes before concluding her speech with: "You are the privileged. You're here. But do you appreciate it?"

I didn't want to be privileged.

I wanted to get out of St. Theresa's, and the solution for escape finally came to me during one of the Mother Superior's Friday sermons: I would break enough rules to be expelled. Then my mother would have to take me back, and the nuns could give my space to one of those deserving girls on the list.

By noon of the following Friday I had collected forty-two demerits and many mournful glances from an assortment of nuns. Did they have to practice those looks before they could take their vows?

My roommates had been at St. Theresa's longer than I and knew how to get around the rules without getting caught. It became my goal to get caught as often as possible, even it if meant having to stay on weekends. I looked upon those weekends as an investment.

Lights out was at nine, and often Alice, a tall girl from Hartford, would get out her small black radio and teach us new dance steps. Except for a floodlight on the wing across from our window, the room was dark. In our identical white nightgowns we'd take turns dancing with Alice, one ear pressed against her ear where the earphone let forth the latest hits. One of us would stand guard by the door and, upon the steady fall of a nun's leather soles in the hallways, hiss softly, and we'd jump into our beds, Alice with her radio, and pull the blankets to our chins. Occasionally, the nun on duty would open the door, a long flashlight in her hand, and I'd feel the light sweeping across the room, across my tightly shut eyes before the nun had convinced herself we were asleep. Once, standing guard, I considered letting the nun catch us dancing, but I didn't because it would involve the others. The girls in my room were all right, but I didn't get too friendly with them since—soon—I'd be leaving anyhow. Instead I wrote long letters to my friend, Jocelynn, who lived in the same apartment building as I and who was the only one to know of my plan to be expelled.

Though I accumulated quite a few demerits by making my bed the wrong way, walking around with my blouse hanging out of my pleated skirt, and reading in the bathroom after the others were asleep, the nuns, after reprimanding me, kept forgiving me. If only I could carry my sum of demerits from one week to the next—a subtotal of kinds—until I reached one hundred. Surely that should be enough. To start with zero demerits every Friday evening was discouraging.

I even began to suspect that the nuns, on purpose, were overlooking things. To test them, I smeared a grape jelly thumbprint across the front of my blouse and paraded it past Mother Catherine, the most beautiful of the nuns, who had a doll's porcelain face and sky-blue eyes, as well as a passion for order and cleanliness. She blinked, her eyes transfixed to the front of my blouse, and then turned away, her slender fingers fumbling for her rosary in the deep folds of her habit. In study hall I tested Mother Beatrice with the same stain *and* dirty fingernails. Again: visible shock but no repercussions.

Perhaps I was breaking the wrong rules, wasting effort on one- or two-pointers when I should have been aiming for something in the range of five or ten.

The end of November Shelly Lambert, who lived in the room next to mine, was caught smoking. On her night table she kept a bronze incense burner in which she'd light cone-shaped pieces that smelled of violets whenever she smoked one of the cigarettes her younger brother smuggled in on visiting days. Rumor had it that Shelly came very close to being expelled; Vicki Meyers heard her cry in the Mother Superior's office, promising she'd never smoke again. That Friday, Shelly, who'd never collected more than four or five demerits, had eighteen. Smoking must have earned her anywhere between ten and fifteen.

Though I hated the smell of tobacco, I took up smoking. One of the day students, Eleanor Peters, bought a pack of Winstons for me, and I practiced in the bathroom before letting myself get caught behind the infirmary by Mother

Abigail. Promptly, she took me to the office of the Mother Superior and left with a worried glance at me after explaining the situation.

"What do you have to say for yourself?" Getting up from the chair behind her desk, the Mother Superior walked toward me, holding the pack of Winstons between her right thumb and forefinger as if afraid the bright red of the package might stain her hands.

I'd never stood this close to her; she looked even bigger than on stage behind that lectern. Staring at the gleaming leather of her black shoes, I waited for her to tell me I'd be expelled.

"You've been a very difficult child so far. Do you know that?"

Should I nod? She might take that as an admission of guilt, and for the nuns guilt was the first step toward redemption.

"Look at me. I asked you a question."

"I didn't know."

The black eyebrows went up. "You've been disobedient, disorderly, disrespectful . . . and you tell me you don't know that?"

I didn't say anything.

"Do you have any idea how unhappy it would make your mother to find out how you've been behaving here? I've held back notifying her, but now. . ." She shook her head. Surely, any moment now she'd start talking about how privileged I was to be here, and how those girls on the outside would give anything to be in my place. Instead she went on about responsibility and attitude and behavior, and about how God forgives even the lowest sinner.

If I didn't stop her, she'd forgive me for smoking and keep

forgiving me for any other rule I might decide to break in the future. "Those girls on the waiting list—I'd be glad to give my place to one of them," I said, hoping she'd agree this might be for the best.

She reached inside her left sleeve and brought out a wad-ded tissue. Sniffling delicately, she dabbed at her nostrils. "Your mother," she finally said, "have you ever considered how hard it is for her to bring you up by yourself? Such a shame she was widowed so young." She stashed the tissue back in the depths of her sleeve. "Of course, you lost your father so early..."

All at once I knew there was no list of deserving girls waiting to get into St. Theresa's; I'd been accepted without delay, and I'd seen empty beds in some of the rooms. Each occupied bed meant six thousand dollars tuition, and the nuns were not about to give that up, regardless how many demerits any of us collected. Inside of me a hot, sour column rose, and I swallowed hard to keep it from my mouth.

"We've made a commitment to your mother to help her with your upbringing," the Mother Superior said as she opened the door for me, "and we intend to do just that."

My head felt curiously light as I walked down the empty hallway. Everyone else was in class. The sound of my shoes against the black and white tiles was like applause, mocking my futile plans of escape.

Such a shame she was widowed so young...
I'd rather be with you than with anyone else...
Lies. All of them.

In the bathroom I ran the cold water until it turned icy. I cupped my hands under the faucet, bent down, and drank for a long time. When I stood up, my nose and chin were wet; in the mirror I watched two drops of water run down my neck.

Such a shame she was widowed so young...

Of course she would have told the nuns that. And they'd believed her. Just as I had believed everything she'd told me.

I wiped my hands against the sides of my skirt and, quickly, left the bathroom. I knew if I waited, if I let myself think, I'd never go through with it. I started running. Opened her office door without knocking.

She was sitting at her desk, one hand holding down the pages of an open book. Through the small window panes the bright afternoon sun slanted, breaking into a pattern of yellow squares on the floor.

"What is it?" She frowned.

I stepped through the tiny particles of dust that floated in the light.

"Yes?"

"I'm—" My voice sounded too loud.

She took off her bifocals. From the hall came the ringing of a bell, announcing the end of classes.

The air felt dry against the inside of my throat. "I don't have a father. I'm—" And then I said it, the word I'd never even tested aloud inside my room at home—"illegitimate" —a word so powerful it filled the office.

At first she didn't believe me. I could tell by the way she looked at me, hard and probing. But I kept staring right back into her eyes until—finally—they turned unforgiving.

Unearned Pleasures

HE WATCHES HER as she pulls on her white cotton pants and fastens her bra, absorbed in that moment of dressing as though her mind has already left his apartment.

He doesn't want her to leave.

"Do you feel guilty when you go home to your husband and child after being with me?"

"No." Smiling at him over her shoulder, she walks to the teak dresser and takes a hairbrush from her handbag.

He has seen her with her husband and child. Last Sunday he parked his car at the end of her street and sat waiting. Her husband came from the house and began raking leaves. Later, a small girl in red overalls ran from the door and jumped into the piles of leaves, laughing as her father picked her up and tossed her into the air. And then she, too, came out, wearing a man's plaid shirt, and stood with her husband, her arm touching his, looking at the child, talking.

He would never tell her how often he drives out to Malden and down the street where she lives, hoping to see her through one of the windows of her old clapboard house. He imagines her rooms filled with books and toys and odd, functional pieces of furniture, easily discarded and replaced. All his furniture he designs himself: low spare lines, teak and rosewood. His office is the largest room of his apartment, a wall of windows facing the Charles River.

"Should I feel guilty?" Standing in front of the mirror, she pulls the brush through her long brown hair. Below her left shoulder blade grows a small mole; her skin stretches over the knobs of her spine.

"I thought you might." He longs to be her confessor, consoling her, understanding her conflict. But there doesn't seem to be a conflict for her. Something is lacking; he desires real suffering—hers—so her pleasures will be earned, so he can be strong and understanding.

"I don't." She brushes her hair with the same concentration she brings to their lovemaking.

One afternoon he followed her car to the tennis courts by the Malden high school and, from a distance, watched her swing her racket at the ball, her attention focused on the game. Though he kept far enough away so she couldn't see him, he had the fear that, should he step onto the court, it would take her time to remember his name.

He wonders if her husband recognizes that same intensity in her when she gets dressed or feeds their child or sits in the same room with him in the evening, reading a book or listening to music. She rarely speaks to him of her husband and child, keeps them separate from her hours with him.

"You still love him?"

In the mirror her blue eyes find his, and as she looks at him, steadily, he wonders if she'll carry this image of him—barechested, leaning against the headboard, covers pulled to his waist—through the week until next Tuesday.

"Yes," she says quietly. "Does that surprise you?"

"A little, perhaps."

"Why?"

He'd like to believe she loves him, although she has never told him so. In the beginning, eight months ago, he worried she might want to leave her husband and child for him; it made him cautious with her, anticipating demands he now doubts he'll ever make.

"Because of your feelings for me," he finally says.

"You ask too many questions."

She comes back to his bed, and he lets her take him into her arms, responds to her kisses, knowing it is this—their joining of pleasures—she wants, not his searching for reasons.

She is one month older than he, but sometimes it seems like years because he can't touch the center of her calm, because she only lets him into her life one afternoon each week, because he needs her more than she seems to need him. If she loved him, there would be remorse, a feeling of betrayal toward her husband. And this is what disturbs him most: that his impact on her is not great enough to make her feel guilty.

"I'm glad you don't feel guilty," he tells her after they've made love; yet, he would like to reassure her, if she felt guilty, that what they have is right for both of them.

But she doesn't appear to need reassurance, and he feels

cheated knowing she might walk away from him this week or the next without suffering, without missing him. Often, at the drawing board, her face superimposes itself on his work, and he stares at the lines of the furniture he designs, powerless to fill those hours of longing with his work. He would like to design a desk for her, or perhaps a rosewood frame for a large mirror, but he hasn't mentioned it to her because he doubts she'll bring anything that's so much a part of him into her house. Besides, it wouldn't fit.

He lives his week inside the boundaries of Tuesdays when she drives into Boston for a sociology class she takes at B.U. and spends the afternoon with him. But even now, as she lies by his side, eyes closed though not asleep, his pleasure in being with her is spoiled by apprehending that, soon, she will get up and leave.

The wind whips a fast pattern of sunlight and branches against the ceiling. Watching the dance of light, he thinks of her child who stays at a neighbor's house on Tuesdays, who is perhaps looking out of a window at the leaves in the wind. Is she, too, thinking of her child? But he doesn't want to ask because then she might notice that it's time for her to go.

Sometimes, alone, he forces his eyes shut and wills her to remember him, at that moment, wherever she might be, even though he knows he's not part of her awareness as her husband and child.

Feeling the slight weight of her body next to him in bed, nothing touching but the side of her left arm against his, he wishes it wouldn't be this easy for her.

Nobody Stocks
Camellias Anymore

YOU STAND IN front of the mirror, Helena, the long reflection of the satin yellowed against the white carnation pinned to your waist. Dark hemline and faint stains. It was white when you stood waiting and felt their eyes on your back. Sometimes people come back after many years. Dirt splatters

from cabs and buses. Don't come out anymore after cleaning. Those modern fluids. Even ruined the veil five years ago. $8.50 for a little white hat. Not the same. They always stare, drivers, passengers, guests. Must look for another Chinese vase. The fourth is almost full, and your fingertips touch the opaque shimmer, cool from within the red. Listen to the voices of the foreign children, Helena, darkeyed chanting below your window, thinfast wrists and voices. Nobody stocks camellias anymore. Special orders only. In the refrigerator they used to last for a week. Just carnations and the uncomfortable stiffness of gladioli. Aspirin. From the table by the door you take your small bag, white plastic beads, made in Taiwan. Hate the smell of liver. You open the clasp, Helena, always

the correct change. The door sucks shut behind you, jerks the bus into motion. The other wedding this afternoon. Across town. 7:32. There, another nickel. Enough, should be no more than three, three-fifty for a cab. When you think of him, you see his face smoothunlined, his hair darkfull. He never grew old for you. One must be ready. You like it, Helena, if there are ushers. Keep your shoulders straight, remember Miss Bannon, a girl's posture is one of

her best assets. Walking down the aisle, your fingertips rest on the borrowed sleeve of a light-blue boy usher. The bride's side, of course. Sometimes the organist begins when you walk down the aisle, Helena, long pumping sounds, and when he stops everybody squints at the silence. Not today. You tilt your head to the left. Thank you, young man. Always a freshly ironed handkerchief, lace, sprinkled with 4711. Seven minutes was the longest. You watched her

wait, Helena, suffering her stiff shoulders. Others waited four, almost five minutes. Never more than seven. Never as long as you before you turned. So much trust walking down an aisle. They don't know how much longer it takes to walk back. Alone with the sound of your shoes against the marble floor past thirty-four rows of pews. Alone, after you loosen your eyes from the camellias on the altar and let the faces in the pews burn their pity into you. But they always came since, came sheepishly running from a side door. How can one ever be sure? A few of them waited too. Nervous shoes, but their shoulders moved. Heads twistedlooked, and that never grapsed your breath, Helena, and stuttered it from you. Listen

to him sing, Helena. Bigbellied fathervoice. Is this the little girl I. Only two bridesmaids. No pets allowed. See the crown of red and white roses in her hair, Helena? Used to be only white. Slow steps. Shoes won't show. Nice posture. Nobody ever plays here comes the bride anymore. You prefer a tenor. The tall woman in front of you moves, Helena, and for a moment you can't see if

he is there, and the skin above your cheekbones tightensburns. Yes. He is. Yes. The chain of insurance remains unbroken. You swallow. The back of your knees steady the bench. We all know that Jesus was

a beautiful man, but not as beautiful as Bill here. Regular M.C., pausing twice during the vows for graysuited pictures from crouched perspectives. Frozen in smiling ceremony. Arranged and again. You wouldn't have liked it, Helena. Fluent hands, see his actor's hands? Listen to his arrogant familiarity. IdoIdoIdo reverberations. You hope

that nobody will laugh at you today. Laughs masked by pity are silent. But you know all about them, Helena. You see them move up and down behind their throats. Let them stare, Helena. Your shoulders will never hurt like that again, nor will their eyes

scorch your back. IdoIdo. Better stock up. Catfood-special Monday. How you can predict their reactions, Helena. Emphasized embarrassed smiles, nods, soles rasping-clicking filing out, safely isolated in contactrubbing against others, pushing. Murmuring of nylonthighs. Those who look away quickly. Impossible to

find white shoes this time of year. You sit down, Helena, waiting for the last of them to leave, for the sound of occupied voices to dissolve in the November gray. Sometimes they are still there when you leave. You'd rather wait until there is only the scattered rice. Four years to fill one swollen. Red laquer. Must buy another vase. You rise, Helena, and the smell of

churches all churches falls off at the arched door, abruptly, the sealed smell of constricted protection, of safemeasured despair. The outside envelops you, and you bend to pick up the familiar ivory shininghardness. Everybody gone. Rigid tears, you polish them against your skirt, Helena,smoothing them against the satin. Symbols of fertility should be soft and yielding. How can anything grow from this rigidity? Still, you take eight as from every wedding and open the clasp. Go

home, Helena, one wedding is enough. Tonight your feet will be blistered. A pretty red, but the heels are too high and the leather still stiff, smelling new. Small steps. Nobody saw them. You need to know for sure if he'll be there, even if you are not. It is not enough to call the minister afterwards. More than that. Breaking the flow of insurance. Fragile obligation. Once you went

to five weddings. Last June and buses would have taken too long. Twenty-three-eighty fare. There would have been six. You were late. Everybody had left. It was called off, last minute. You never found out if it was because you broke the chain of insurance. One weak link. Perhaps she called if off. Too much of a chance. He might not come if you are not there to make sure. They

like to play on the stone steps in front of your building, Helena, while they wait for you. They never laugh or look away with their throats moving. Children like to see brides. They become very silent. When you

get home, you will let your fingers run through the rice of many weddings, and your hands will sink into the polished quicksand of fertility. You will empty today's grains into the fourth vase, ornate lacquer, sifting it with the rice of togetherness, of disillusion and contentment, of compromise and sterility. Two for forty-five cents. Small cans. High in protein and liversmell. No need to buy the paper Thursday. Check the weddings in the library copy. Seven-eighty

but the old spots stay, fading deeper into the yellowed satin. Loose around your waist. Tomorrow you will iron it, Helena, and put it back on the pink hanger padded with foam rubber. Your carnation might last. Drop an aspirin into the water before you put it into the refrigerator. And if you wear your new shoes for half an hour every evening, you will break them in. Your feet won't hurt so much next

Saturday. The run in your stocking doesn't show. Only you know. One must be ready. Sometimes people just get lost and come back after many years.

Windows

THROUGH THEIR WINDOW Paul could see them sitting around the table, eating, and as he moved to the right into the taller clumps of grass, he saw the woman carrying a pitcher of milk in from the kitchen. Their names he didn't know, only their faces and how they looked at one another with kindness. Damp grass covered his sneakers, soaked the cuffs of his chinos. Reaching back, he adjusted his pack; he could always tell when his son fell asleep: the backpack became heavier. Lifting it from the bottom, he straightened Michael's legs through the openings so they wouldn't get cramped.

The woman turned her face to the man and smiled. Amy used to look at him like that when they first were married. He wished he could tell them that tomorrow he would leave, that his truck was packed. His gardening tools were tied to the back, the crates with his strawberry plants stacked behind the driver's side, easy to get to for watering. He'd secured the yellow ceramic lamp between the two cowhide suitcases on top of the red pick-up.

For a week Amy had been packing. Most of his clothes she'd given to the Salvation Army. "You'll wear suits from now on." She seemed as happy about moving as she'd been the first few months after Michael was born, when she'd held him for hours, playing with his hands, talking and singing to him.

Michael shifted without waking. Time to go. Paul felt reluctant to leave the people he'd come to know so well over the last years. It didn't matter that they didn't know him, didn't know of him. Turning from the light in the window, he started down the hill past the open field with the boulders, past the clearing where the white trailer used to stand. Again he wondered what had happened to the young couple and their child who'd once lived here. One evening last fall their windows had remained dark; the next day he'd found a sign: *For Sale, Burke Agency*, nailed to the birch in front of the trailer. A month later someone bought it and hauled it away.

Soon Michael would become too large to be carried like this. Paul had bought the baby carrier when his son was four months old to take him along on his walks after dinner. Sometimes Amy asked him to bring back a couple of Milky Ways. He got them at the corner store on the way home. While she ate them, he undressed Michael, put a double diaper on him for the night, and laid him, stomach down, into the crib. Funny, how he liked to fall asleep lying on his stomach, arms tight against his sides, knees tucked under so his butt stuck in the air. Yet, early in the morning, when Paul checked in on him, he'd be lying on his back, arms flung open like a parachuter.

Yesterday they'd sold his crib to a young couple expecting their first in September. "He's old enough to sleep in a real bed once we get to Massachusetts," Amy had said. Her parents had bought a house for them, though Paul would have rather rented an apartment. The photo they'd sent showed a white cape with green shutters and two dogwood trees in front. *The new house.* It was all Amy talked about ever since she'd convinced him to work for her father. First Paul didn't want to go. Until he saved enough for a down payment on the farm he wanted to buy some day, he felt content working at Benson's Farm Supply.

Weighing grain for Ned Stimpson one afternoon, he'd seen Amy for the first time. She'd come into the store, looking for a handpainted flower pot. Everything about her was soft. Soft and round. Her face. The pink circle of her mouth. Her breasts. Arms. Even the curls of her blond hair. He told her all they had were regular clay pots, and after looking through the rack with seed packages, glancing a few times in his direction, she left and got into a red Mustang.

Two days later, walking past the fire station, he recognized her car parked in front of the diner across the street. Through one of the windows he saw her sitting alone in a booth. He went in, sat down at the counter, and ordered a cup of soup though he wasn't particularly hungry. After a while he went to Amy's table and asked if she'd ever found that flower pot.

She smiled. "I'm still looking. I might have to wait until I get home to buy one."

"Where's that?"

"Massachusetts. I'm a sophomore at Kansas State." She invited him to sit down and told him about her classes. "Chemistry is the worst. One of those dumb science requirements..." She hadn't decided on her major yet. "At first I thought of anthropology, but that's too boring.

He ordered coffee and drank it slowly while she talked about her teachers, the crowded dorms, her parents. Her father had his own company. Packing materials.

"It's all he cares about." She ran her fingertips through her short hair, fluffing it out. "He'd walk over anybody to get what he wants."

Suddenly embarrassed for her, he looked down at his hands.

"You get along with your parents." More a statement than a question.

He nodded. "Your mother—you must miss her."

"She's not like me. She's pretty."

"So are you."

She shrugged. "She's always after me to lose weight. Wear different clothes. Do something about my hair. She spends hours on her hair and makeup. The rest of the day she's busy with her charities. Always has meetings. It doesn't leave her much time to write to me." She swirled her coke with the pink straw. "Not that I'd want her to."

She said almost the same thing five months later when her parents refused to come to the wedding. "I wouldn't want them here anyhow." But she wouldn't look into Paul's eyes.

When he opened his arms to her, she clung to him, and he believed he could make up for the love she hadn't been given.

They found an apartment, four rooms on the second floor

of 53 Warner Street, only a few blocks from Benson's. Amy quit school and insisted on selling her car, using the money for a plaid love seat with matching chairs and a red rug for the living room. Paul's parents gave them his old maple bedroom set, and his Uncle Francis brought over a driftwood table with a Plexiglas top. Through the Sears catalog Amy ordered a color TV console and a pillow embroidery kit of swans against a red background. She began working on it the day it arrived. For his twenty-third birthday she gave Paul two cowhide suitcases and, for the first time, he wondered why he didn't have the desire to travel.

It took him several months to notice that, where before she had complained about her parents and college, she now found things wrong with the apartment, the clothes he wore, the time he spent cultivating the small garden in back. She doesn't mean it, he thought, trying not to let her words hurt him. Yet, sometimes he felt angry, and it made him uneasy. To make up for it, he gave her gifts: candy or magazines. One evening he stopped at the flower shop on the way home and chose six red roses.

"Surprise," he said, opening the door.

Her bare feet on the smudged top of the Plexiglas table, she sat in front of the TV. "You're late." She glanced at him, then back to the set.

"I got some flowers for you."

"I'm making hot dogs the third time this week, and you're throwing out money on flowers." Her face flushed. "How much?"

A commercial for a car dealer came on. With a trust-me-smile and insincere cheeks a heavy salesman promised low prices and three-month guarantees on all used cars. Too much orange tint in the picture.

111

"Well?" she asked.

A wrinkled corner of the unfinished embroidery kit hung from between a pile of magazines.

"You don't have to stay in this dump all day. Junk. All we have is junk. Hand-me-downs from your precious family. And you buy roses."

Through the paper he felt the stems pressing into his palm. Suddenly he found it difficult to swallow. Abruptly he turned and ran down the stairs. On the back porch he dropped the flowers into the trash can. He walked away from the house and kept walking until he was too tired to think. It became the first of many walks he would take in the next years. Sometimes he'd see a family around the dinner table, smiling and talking. Why couldn't Amy be like that? He'd always thought people were unhappy for a reason: illness, death, unemployment. But Amy needed no reason; her discontent seemed to come from within like breathing.

For a while after Michael's birth, Paul thought everything would be all right now that they'd become a real family. He saw the delight Amy took in the new baby, the way she smiled when she bent over him. She posed Michael for dozens of snapshots and ordered extra copies to send to her parents. But soon she seemed relieved when Paul bathed and changed their son. Only in the last weeks, while getting ready for the move to Massachusetts, had her enthusiasm returned. He still didn't understand why she wanted to go back or why her father had offered him a job in his company.

"Maybe she's been homesick all along," he told his parents when he said good-bye. "Maybe it's for the best." He tried to sound more hopeful than he felt, and his mother gently touched his right cheek with the back of her hand.

There's always room for you with us," his father said. "Remember that now."

Two hours out of Kansas the ceramic lamp fell off the truck when one of the ropes between the suitcases came undone. As well as he could, Paul cleaned the broken pieces off the road and tied the dented lamp shade on top of the maple dresser. After that he checked the ropes every time they stopped. At night they stayed in small motels where Amy would talk of her parents' house, of high school friends she'd invite for dinner, of the playmates she'd find for Michael. The last time Paul tightened the ropes, they'd come within eighty miles of the house her parents had bought.

The houses on Star Road—ranches and capes—looked almost alike: some had garages or breezeways, three trees instead of two. As Paul climbed from the truck, his knees were stiff. Under his arms the blue T-shirt felt sticky. The August heat shimmered thickly above the asphalt of the narrow driveway.

Slowly, Amy got out on her side, pulling her wrinkled print skirt down. "It looks smaller than in the photo."

Inside the house was clean. Clean and empty. Blue shag covered the floors of the living room and three bedrooms; the kitchen had striped wallpaper and white appliances. While Paul unloaded the truck, Amy kept watching the end of the street, promising Michael his grandparents should be there any minute. But they didn't come until after eight that evening, and when they looked at the pieces of furniture, dusty from days on the truck, Paul realized how out of place they seemed on the thick carpet. He, too, felt out of place with his dirty hands and clothes.

When Amy's father extended his manicured hand, Paul

quickly wiped his right palm against the side of his jeans before shaking it. Amy's mother, small and slim, wore a light blue dress and matching coat; she kept the coat on during their brief visit. Paul wished she wouldn't keep glancing at the two rolls of flesh between Amy's skirt and pink halter, and he felt oddly protective.

"Can't you say hello to your grandparents?" Amy smiled as she tried to pull Michael forward, but he shrank back and hid behind Paul's leg, sucking the middle finger of his left hand.

"Doesn't he talk yet?" Amy's mother asked.

"He's usually quiet," Paul said. "Especially with strangers."

Amy laughed nervously. "Not that you'll be strangers for long." She offered her parents coffee, iced tea, ginger ale. "Or I could drive to the store and get something you like."

They said they couldn't stay.

She didn't stop smiling, not even when the brown Cadillac pulled out of the driveway, not until Paul put his arms around her. "I thought they wanted me to come back." She began to cry.

He held her close, running one hand up and down her soft back. "We have each other."

In the morning the skin around her eyes was puffy, and she stayed indoors, afraid one of the neighbors might see her like this. Paul let Michael help him set his strawberry plants into the ground. Though the backyard was small, he figured he could at least plant some corn and tomatoes next spring.

Saturday they drove into Boston and bought two suits for him at Filene's: one the same shade of gray as the one Amy's father had worn, the other blue with a vest. The black shoes

Amy chose for him felt uncomfortable after years of wearing boots and sneakers. Though he tried to break them in over the weekend, they still were stiff on Monday morning when he stood in the paved parking lot of Moore, Inc., watching Amy and Michael drive away in the truck. He hesitated before entering the double glass door, feeling conspicuous in his unfamiliar clothes. Amy's father introduced him to men and women who wore their clothes with ease, who smiled at him and said they hoped he'd like his new job. Almost instantly he forgot their names.

At home the kitchen counter and table stayed hidden under boxes and stacks of dishes and towels; in the bedroom stood three laundry baskets with unfolded clothes; the unfinished embroidery kit lay in the drawer with Michael's undershirts.

By two in the afternoon Paul usually was tired, more so than he'd ever felt working at Benson's until nine on Thursdays. His back ached from sitting behind a desk, and he felt dizzy from trying to take in all the new information. Climate-controlled, the building stayed at an even sixty-eight degrees. Since it had no windows, he didn't know if it was raining or if the sun was shining. Though he saw Amy's father every day at work, they'd only been invited to their house for dinner once, and whenever Amy asked her mother to meet her for lunch or shopping, she was too busy.

"The neighbors are snobs," Amy decided. "Probably because of the truck."

Calls to her high school friends resulted in one strained cocktail party. Paul wore his blue suit; Amy bought a green dress with a flared skirt. Three couples in jeans came, sat around Uncle Francis's Plexiglas table, eating cheese puffs and drinking champagne punch. A quarter to ten they left.

Paul found little pleasure in his evening walks. Roads were short and paved, houses built side by side. Beyond— the highways and shopping centers. No hills. No open fields where he could feel the earth soft under his shoes. On the asphalt his feet tired quickly. Yet, he kept his habit of walking after dinner, carrying Michael on his back, feeling best when his son linked his thin arms around his neck.

But in November it became too chilly to take Michael along, and Paul waited until his son was asleep before leaving the house. The first evening he walked alone, he felt strange without the familiar weight on his back. Stepping from one wide circle of light of one street lamp to the next, he passed houses with closed drapes. He wondered where the people from the white trailer had moved, if they, too, felt out of place. The first time he'd seen them, the woman had been in her last month of pregnancy. Through the window of the trailer he'd seen her sitting in a rocking chair, her swollen body moving in and out of the narrow frame with the swaying of the chair. An old Chevy drove up, and a short man in overalls got out. The woman left her chair, and they embraced by the door. Paul watched them the day they brought their baby home from the hospital. Michael was two months old then. As both children learned to crawl and walk, he sometimes thought how nice it would be to take Michael down there and say, *Hi, my name's Paul Ritchie. This here's my son, Michael.* He'd sit with the man on the wooden steps in front of the trailer, watching the children play. The woman would bring out some coffee or beer, smiling first at her husband and then at him. But something kept him back.

Only after they'd left, did he go close enough to walk across the brown, matted grass where the trailer had stood.

From behind the station wagon came the high-pitched bark of a small dog. A white poodle darted out. At home his parents had a dog, a brown mutt from the pound. Once Michael was older, it would be good for him to have a dog. Paul crouched, stretching out his right hand. Cautiously, the dog circled him, then stopped barking to sniff his fingers. From a window someone whistled. A door opened. The poodle ran toward a red ranch.

Straightening, Paul felt cold and tired. Suddenly he wanted to be home though it felt odd to think of the house Amy's parents had paid for as home. Cutting across the lawn between two garages, he walked past swing sets and sand-boxes. The street lamps didn't reach this far. Here the ground was soft and made him think of the open fields back home, those long furrows lying straight under the moon like the ribs in the corrugated cardboard that Amy's father manufactured. The longing for a farm of his own made his throat ache.

From behind him came a sudden voice. "What are you—" Something struck his head.

Heavily he fell forward. Darkness. Other voices. A rushing in his ears like water running down a drain. Flashlights. Then a hand—helping him up, steadying him. A uniform.

"You all right?" The policeman asked.

"... so when the dog kept barking, I watched him from the kitchen... kept looking at our house... across the Anderson's driveway and I called Bill ... followed him until we caught him by the Miller's bedroom window ..."

Paul shook his head, trying to clear it.

"Did you see him look into the window?" the police officer asked a woman in a bathrobe.

She hesitated. "Not really. I ran outside when Mr. Baldwin started shouting." Her flashlight shone right into Paul's face, and he blinked. "What were you doing back there?"

He tried to see her face, but the light in his eyes was too bright. "A short cut. I—"

"Peeping Tom," one of the men shouted. "Don't waste your time being nice to him."

Paul rubbed the back of his head with his right hand. It stung. "I was trying to—a short cut. To Star Road. I live there."

"You could have gotten hurt." The woman lowered her flashlight. "This time I won't press charges for tresspassing, but don't do it again."

He tried to nod and, without knowing why, suddenly recalled a toy he'd owned as a child: a fuzzy bear with a rope in its mouth, a wind-up toy that turned in a tight circle. Until it stopped.

"Don't let him off that easy," someone said.

"I'll take you home," the policeman said and, when Paul tried to object, he insisted, "Don't want you getting into any more trouble tonight."

Stiffly, Paul sat in the police car, and when it let him off at the end of his driveway, he stood and watched the tail lights disappear down the street. For an instant he wanted to follow their glow. Amy would have heard the car. How could he possibly explain? Slowly, he turned and walked into the house. From the living room came the pitched voices and laugh track of the TV.

"Look at these." Amy was leafing through a catalog. The

right sleeve of her blue nightgown fell back to her elbow as she extended an opened page and pointed to a set of tall glasses. "Jordan's has them on sale this week, and—"

"There's been some trouble." His voice sounded hoarse. Unfamiliar.

"The same kind of glasses that my mother has. If we ordered two dozen, we could have a party for the neighbors."

"I don't know how it happened, but—"

"Maybe that's what we should have done right after we moved in—given a party for the neighbors. They probably expected us to invite them. While I was waiting for them to do something."

His hands felt cold. Damp. He rubbed them together.

"They're one-third off." Her voice had that enthusiastic ring that came with new beginnings. *New husband. New baby. New house. New glasses.* "And if we get two dozen, we'll have extras in case some of them break."

He nodded and stepped next to the window. Pushing the drapes aside with his right hand, he pressed his forehead against the cool glass.

"...and I saw some printed invitations at the drug store, you know, for housewarming parties, and I thought..."

In a second floor window across the street a light came on and then went off again, suddenly, as though someone had found himself in the wrong room.